Vandelier's Song

& 

Ten Other Short Stories

Vandelier's Song

& 10 Other Short Stories

Uffe Berggren

English version from the Swedish original by Uffe Berggren.

Cover photo: Uffe Berggren

Print history for Swedish editions: : Published 2004 in Swedish as "Vandeliers sång". ReaKom: ISBN 91-975104-1-6. It is still possible to purchase a print version, as well as an e-book, from 2017: ISBN 9789176995273.

Publisher: BoD – Books on Demand, Stockholm, Sweden

Print : BoD – Books on Demand, Norderstedt, Germany

ISBN: 9789179698959

Vandelier's Song

& 10 Other Short Stories

Contents

The Home Coming 7

Fatz is the Greasiest 13

In the Greyhound Depot 23

You're Looking at the Next President 40

The Witch Master of Self-pity 56

Drugstore 70

Sunday Morning 83

An Unusual Day, Judy! 98

Roses & Perfume 112

Not Much of a Smile 127

Vandelier's Song 142

Post Script 156

The Home Coming

Ella steps down from the yellow bus in a cloud of stale diesel fumes aggressively spreading in the quivering heat. The sun sparkles in the dust along the sides of the bus, as if thousands of minimal mirrors are fixed all along the bus side, just to get this bus to appear somewhat brighter.

On the stairs of the bus station sits Crazy Harry. He grins between two saliva stripes slowly crawling down the stubble chin. He has not changed.

"Hey, Harry!" she says, "how are you holding up?"

Harry stares blankly, does not seem to recognise her. He squints into the sun. He and the bus station look the same as four years ago.

"Girl," Crazy Harry says, "dog girl!"

He grins even wider and is clumsily flapping his arms. Like he is trying to fly up towards her. Or even greeting her. It is hard to tell.

"Nah?" says Ella, "yes, I always had dogs with me. It is right! Now I have no dog."

Why is she telling him that? Does he understand?

Ella looks around. No one has come to meet her. The sun is sitting so low that it makes her squint like Crazy Harry when she gazes along the road towards the farm. Nothing is to be seen there, nothing that is moving anyway.

Inside the dusty old bus station there is old Vera Bradley still standing behind the counter. As long as Ella can remember, Vera has been working there. Vera has aged, unlike Crazy Harry. Mainly through that her cheeks are hanging even lower than in the past.

Vera looks up from her packages when Ella comes in.

"My, oh my, look who's coming here, Martin Parks girl! The youngest if my old eyes doesn't deceive me. Jenny, no, Gabriella was your name?" Vera Bradley says and smiles so wide her face splits into hundreds of wrinkles.

"Right," Ella says and is definitely sensing a lump growing in her throat.

For the first time in years any one outside work recognises her, or knows who she is. Now, these two guys recognised her in a matter of minutes!

"Long time since you were home, right honey?"

"Yes, it has been a few years," Ella mumbles.

"At home on vacation?" Vera wonders and gazes intently at Ella with her piercing icy blue eyes.

"Nah, I quit!"

"Couldn't you take it?" Vera Bradley asks with some anxiety in her voice.

"Oh yes, but ..."

"I see! The old place still has its lure. Where did you live, in New York?"

"Yes, and in Montreal."

"With your mother then?"

"No, but she lives in Montreal," Ella replies and is

Vandelier's Song

noticing that Vera does not keep up with what is happening.

"Oh yes, I knew it was a big city. What did you do there then?"

"Working at museums as a guard, waitressing, delivering mail and such," Ella says.

Ella feels like she is being cross-examined. Then she remembers that Vera Bradley, of course, serves as the village's news agency.

"Well," Vera Bradley says and ponders on it, "and now you're home!"

Vera looks at Ella over her horn rimmed glasses. Vera's grey hair is like aged wood in the harsh bright sunshine from the windows.

"Yes, it seems that way!"

Outside a car horn is honking. Ella gazes out the window and recognises her father's old truck. A young, good-looking guy is sitting in it. At first glance she does not recognise him.

"But, it's Jimmy!" Ella yells and rushes out into the blinding sun out on the dusty street.

She hugs the young man while he is still trying to step down from the truck's cabin. When he is standing beside her she notices that her little brother is now a head taller than her. She has to tilt her head back to look at him. Previously, it was he who had to do that tilting movement. He is a little embarrassed she notes. He looks hesitatingly at her.

"So tiny you have become," he says, "you're so pale. How are you doing?"

"Tired," she answers with a faint smile.

"Okay, get in, so we can be on our way home," Jimmy says.

They sit in silence for a while as a puzzlingly familiar landscape sweeps past them on both sides. Ella notices that Jimmy looks at her a few times, as if trying not to let her know that he is looking.

"Seems to have been a tough journey."

"Yes," she responds, and glances at him.

Imagine that her little brother has grown and become such a tall and handsome guy! Where has time gone?

"How is mother?" he asks.

"Oh well, she's okay. She thrives well in life, as you could have suspected," Ella says.

"She's still working at the museum?"

"Yes," she replies."

"Thought of going to visit her in the fall," Jimmy says.

"She'll like that!"

"Might be fun to meet her."

"How old are you now, Jimmy?" Ella asks and looks at him and squints a bit.

"Eighteen," he replies.

"And a danger to the girls," Ella laughs, "you've really grown up, little brother!"

"Well, I don't know about that," Jimmy says, a trifle embarrassed.

They sit quiet for some time. Ella notes that she still recognises every house, every bend in the road, well, almost every tree and patch of the road.

It was not that long ago anyway!

"You got my letter?"

"Yes, Dad was happy, of course. Over you coming home for a while, that is."

"Will be great to see him."

"Because you're not going to stay? You still hate this place?" Jimmy wonders.

Ella glances at him. He is no longer a small boy with a runny nose. Now he is an grown man. Looks more adult than she is feeling herself.

"You can't tell Dad!" she pleads.

"What then?"

"What I'm going to tell you," she says.

"Okay!"

He glances quickly at her. Then fixes his eyes again on the road. There is not much to watch, but it is that way when you are driving a car. Therefore, he does it.

"You see, I got pregnant down there," she says very silently.

"Well," says Jimmy and is still staring straight ahead. His jaw muscles seem unnaturally taut.

"You're not embarrassed, huh?" she wonders.

"Nah," he replies without looking at her.

"There was a man I did not really like. So it was ..."

"You'll deliver it here at home?" Jimmy wonders.

"No, I got rid of it."

Now it seems definite. Now it's over and she has even told it to someone she can relate to. She is sad, but not as stunned as before.

"You, ... okay!" Jimmy says.

Ella is convinced that he is blushing.

"You certainly have grown up, little brother!" Ella mumbles.

She pats his arm. He turns towards her and smiles. The sun comes in from her side of the car, so he squints slightly towards her.

"I was planning to rest and think," she says.

"Okay!"

"But Jimmy, don't tell Dad anything! He will just get worried," she pleads.

"Not a word!" Jimmy promises.

She is feeling more alert. She is not alone. Now she has a little brother who is big enough to share her worries.

"I wonder," she says, "have you bought a new dog?"

Fatz is the greasiest

There are good restaurants, that are bad and bad restaurants, that are great. There are even many places that do not really deserve to be called restaurants at all. Fatz is one of those. Fatz does not hesitate to take a deep breath at calling itself a restaurant, but not far from it. Fatz is not far from calling itself a restaurant, but far from being a good restaurant.

It is primarily a place to stay a while, grab a bite to eat and save a few dollars before you move on to the next place, where ever you are heading.

Morego Avenue runs along the highway from San Francisco down to Berkeley. At LaSalle Street sits Montclair Center, which is a little insidious suburban center. And on LaSalle Street is Fatz.

There are other restaurants on Morego, but Fatz is the greasiest. Fatz is owned by Jim Haggerty, who once upon a time was nick-named Fatz. He has lost a lot of weight since those days and is rather skinny now, but the name still lives on. In some ways this is a disappointment to the guests who walk into Fatz and for some reason want to talk to the proprietor. When introduced to Jim Haggerty something they sense that something is lacking. Sure, you might fathom that Haggerty has been a big fat guy at some time. But, at Fatz there has to be a fat proprietor. The ordinarily sized Haggerty does not make him as an owner anymore. Luckily enough people nowadays rarely ask for the proprietor. That is not the kind of clientele they have at Fatz. The ones coming in nowadays don't ask for much. They can handle that Haggerty isn't as fat as he once used to be, especially in his younger days. It's the ordinary customers, the regulars if you want to call them that, they can cope with the way things are at the moment. For others it is way harder.

At Fatz you can have a meal without ruining yourself. Most people having their meals at Fatz work within the Montclair Center. Some argue that it's good for your economy to have your meals at Fatz, but it might be worse for gastronomy and your looks. But, you shouldn't trust them too much. There is always a lot of gossip travelling around about every food-joint. That's half the charm; the rumors are half of the pleasure when coming here.

Reba adjusts her cap and gives Steve, the Chinese kid who's always teasing her, a scolding. She makes a quick glance into the mirror and she doesn't really object to what she is seeing there, a heart-shaped face with a skin tone like milk chocolate. She can't se much of her hair below her cap, but always crops it very short.

A random observer gazing at Reba might think that life is good. It's a pleasure looking at her, even if she herself sometimes thinks that her appearance leaves very much to be wanted. But she looking good in that mockery of a hat Haggerty thinks she should wear on her head in order to represent Fatz in a pleasing manner.

14

That's the way it is with Reba, her looks are good, but on the ordinary side. She would look alright in almost anything. That is a trait she doesn't really appreciate to its full extent.

"They're just passing by," Reba sighs regarding her image in the mirror and finally makes a face of distaste. "If they were living here, they would be home by now!"

They have seen to it that they are leaving for somewhere else around the outskirts of the city. They have had enough sense to avoid this part. Either is it too expensive, or not fashionable enough. So, there is a special kind of people in the neighborhood.

They're not the ones having a meal at Fatz.

Reba is like said before not content with her own image in the mirror. She wonders why no one else looks at her like she is looking at herself. Men do not really stand in line. Not that it would necessarily be much more fun then, but it would at least be some kind of change. At least.

"Reba, you wont grow more beautiful by looking at yourself in the mirror," Steve teases her.

She smiles, he is always laughing at her and winking at her in a flirtatious manner.

"Steve, how old are you really?"

Reba is coming out from behind the counter. She moves some glasses into the shelf where they use to stand.

"Twenty-two".

Steve looks at her interrogatively.

"I'm twenty-three, did you know that?" Reba says.

Steve looks at her with a somewhat intense stare, smiling a bit.

"Wow, almost an old lady!" Steve says, winking at her.

"Watch out so I don't feed you a knuckle-sandwich! But, you look so childish I'd better not." Reba says.

She giggles some, like she had uttered something really funny. That's the way she's feeling anyway. Whatever that means.

"You'd better. You know all Chinese are masters of Kung Fu?"

Steve clenches his fists and strikes a pose with his feet wide astride.

"No, really?"

She is waiting, but steps up closer to Steve.

"Sure." Steve laughs.

Steve relaxes his pose, continuing to smile at her, like he always does.

Reba laughs and pinches his cheek.

"Yo, Steve, you don't seem like any of them ordinary burger flippers. Don't you do a whole range of other stuff?"

"You could say that".

Steve keeps on polishing the counter. Suddenly its is like he seems very interested in this job.

"Maybe I shouldn't even be guessing, but rather ask you up front what do you think?"

"If you don't want to guess, let me tell you instead", he says.

Steve looks at her, still keeping on polishing the

counter. He checks if Haggerty is on his way back onto the premises.

"I'm proud guessing your secret," says Reba.

She leans towards the counter.

"It's no secret, I make photographs and do a bit of writing", Steve tells her.

"You know pictures of animals in the sunset, forests, the sea and halfway pretentious nature romantic texts to go along with them."

"Aren't you proud of what you do?"

She gazes at him with a somewhat forced and introvert smile.

"It's more like it is not as easy making a living doing them kind of things. No one has shown any interest in buying text and pictures in a while now. That's why I've become interested in the restaurant business. People have to eat and then there is need for guys like me to take care of their dirty cutlery and plates".

"But, what a pity!"

She is taking a chance; she doesn't know if that is what he wants to hear. It's not what she wanted to say. Maybe somewhere in between instead. She doesn't know if it is important to please, that's not really her style. To be honest ,she really doesn't know what her style is. She sighs.

"With such a talent like mine, you mean? Bah, I think it's a good experience. I don't have to run around trying to peddle pictures and texts for a while. Some sort of vacation with salary, if you see it that way."

"How long have you been at it?" Reba wonders.

"Let's see, almost a year. I like it, but I'll quit next month. It's fall in the mountains by then. Then Steve packs his backpack full of film, paper and cameras and hits the road with sleeping bag and tent to catch "the passing of the seasons"."

"I hope you'll get some good pictures," Reba says.

Sure, it's just a thing that you say, but Reba is sincerely hoping that it will work out fine for Steve so he is able to make a living, and then the pictures have to be good enough to sell.

"The question is if anybody wants to buy them!"

"Sure they will."

"Maybe", he mumbles.

Steve looks at her like he wants to remember every shift of the expressions in her face.

"How about you then?" Steve continues. "Will you keep on serving here at Fatz for the remainder of your life?"

He smirks towards Reba, like he knows that she really has bigger plans.

He should only know, Reba thinks, that I have no clue to what I'm going to even tomorrow!

"Not really, but I have no detailed plans for the future", Reba mutters.

Reba smiles at Steve, as to show him how vague a future she has.

"Would you like to go along with me up into the mountains this fall?" he asks. "You could easily fix a new job if you don't like sleeping outdoors?"

"Do you really want me to tag along", she asks. "What

about the rent? I do have a room, you know. A lot of gear too, what about that?"

"Pay the rent two months in advance. Then you might change your mind, or keep on watching nature. You don't need to make any life-changing decisions. Soon there will be wintertime in the mountains and we have to go to where it is warmer. It's all about some weeks, maybe a month."

"You mean you really want me to tag along?"

Why? It's like she can't grasp what he is saying. Like she doesn't want to listen to the words he is using, like she wants to hear that she misunderstands and keep on staying here with her miserable life.

"Maybe we can have a lot of fun together," says Steve with a short chuckle.

Like he really wants to say something completely different. Like he is talking to her in a language he is expecting her to understand. She wonders if she does that, if he says the things she suspects he does. She's not that sure, but it doesn't make any big difference anymore. It's not the most important.

"You mean in the sleeping-bag?" she asks and to her disappointment she notices that she gives a little laugh, a bit nervously.

She not fond of that nervous, prude side in herself, but usually she comforts herself by muttering that she grew out of it.

There are a lot of things she is hoping will become different, just as she gets a bit older.

Now she can't wait much longer to get older, the

years have passed rapidly enough as it is. Maybe it's not only the years she's lacking, but also the experiences that come along with every year older she gets.

"Not necessarily, but you're fun talking to", he says and continues "It's mostly because I like working with you I have stayed here as long as three months. The other places I worked I only endured a couple of weeks each."

"Okay!"

Reba gazes at him.

"Okay, I'll tag along with you if you promise that there is a possibility to slide into your sleeping-bag if I feel like it." Reba sighs.

As recently as yesterday she'd become worried hearing herself saying something like that. Now it seems like the most natural thing in the world. Like the world has changed.

She doesn't understand herself. Something is happening and she doesn't master it, she doesn't even master herself.

She's feeling a bit high by all this news. All these new things happening to her.

"Sure, I'm more than willing to be surprised!"

Steve is staring at her. If someone else had said what he just said, or stared at her in this way, she would truly be worried. Now it doesn't seem that dangerous, it seems cute in a way. She doesn't get why she thinks it is.

"Sounds good!" Reba giggles; though somewhere deep inside her she's a little bit worried.

It frightens her that Steve has such an easy way of handling profoundly loaded words. Still, she doesn't want to get scared, not right now. It seems like it is a nice time and that a bunch of changes are on their way. She has a craving for change. Life's been so boring for such a long time now.

"When can you leave?"

Steve looks right at her and his eyes are so dark it's hard to grasp what he's thinking. Maybe you can't do that even with people with brighter eyes, she ponders.

"Well, I don't know, you said a month?

Reba knows that it doesn't matter when he wants to leave. She doesn't care about Fatz. She could quit right now. Just put her rag down and walk out. But, you're not supposed to do that kind of thing. At least if you would like to give the world the appearance of you being a trustworthy citizen with plans for the future and a clear goal for the rest of life.

"Exactly."

"Then I'm in!"

Reba gives Steve a hug.

"Good, that's settled then!"

Steve replicates her hug and breaks up her hug. He takes a step back, looks at her and then shakes his head, without any contempt.

"But Haggerty will go crazy of course, he's gonna start yelling that Fatz is going bankrupt and that's our fault." Reba rambles on.

"It's going down anyway? Hardly anyone comes here anymore."

Steve gives her a poke at the waist.

"But look, the first guests of the evening!"

Steve leaves for the kitchen. Reba turns towards the couple just entering the door. They are eyeing the premises.

"Table for two?" Reba asks with a broad smile.

The couple turns towards her and smiles back!

In the Greyhound Depot

There's something special about the depots of the Greyhound lines. They are regular life in miniature. They are the heart of the countryside's contacts with the rest of the world.

Just now a metal shining bus arrived. The passengers stepped out of the bus and went into the depot to wait for a friend coming to pick them up, or to wait for the next bus taking them further.

Just like at a railway station there was a movement of change inside the building. Local people were hanging around inside. They were looking at the travellers. Studying their disoriented gazes and trying to figure out what the travellers were heading for. But, just after a few moments they had categorised the travellers and returned to what they had been doing. Some of them seemed to be primarily occupied with smoking. Others were reading. It was an ordinary night. It was late, but not so late that all life had ceased to exist in the waiting area of the bus depot.

In a quiet manner there was something in the air, something almost foreboding a promise. What exactly was promised wasn't quite clear. A lot of people were still waiting for travellers or for one of the approaching buses.

There's something absolute about waiting areas. They

are the hubs where people change lanes in order to get closer to somewhere else. It might reveal new possibilities, or it might bring catastrophes. The biggest catastrophes we really do tend to carry within ourselves, where we harbour the raging forest fires, the tumbling skyscrapers, the all too bloody knives and the run over kids.

Our fantasy is cruel enough to envision what will happen if we don't look out. We can't do much about it. We are forced to live with it. Fantasy is a wonderful ally, but a cruel enemy.

The door to the bus depot swung open with a throbbing bounce, like it was danger ahead. But nobody entered. The door's automatic shutters slowly closed it again. Then a crack was opened. Now, all the attention of the people in the waiting area was spotted on the door.

The waiting area came to a stand still, like all people present in the area kept heir breath waiting for somebody to enter through that door. Of course nobody really kept his or her breath. But, it seemed like the entire spacy room was in a breathless state of waiting.

The entrance door swinging open without anybody entering is a challenge of destiny. Who would be so bold that he opens a door completely in vein? Who really wants to create expectations he or she can't live up to?

Who knows what could be found on the other side of the door. It might be that it is nastier on the other side of the door than on the one you're already in. The bad thing is that you won't know that from the start. You have to take the leap into the abyss each and every time. It's a challenge, but at the same time so gruesome that you'd rather not accept it. That initiates new hardships. That frightens you to the degree that you realize you had better leave that door alone rather than opening it and face the adventure.

Doors have that peculiarity that they are borders between different rooms, between outside and inside, between men and thoughts, between the persons we are and the ones we long to be. Now, here was a shut door and there was something on the other side of that shut door. That something would probably show itself very soon. But it took a while. It took a long time. It took so long time before anything happened that the people waiting started to loose interest in that door.

If you have to wait for too long for something your interest disappears out of you, sooner or later. That's exactly what happened. Four travellers in various ages and with different numbers of suitcases had just entered from the bus that had arrived a couple of minutes earlier. Nobody of the newly arrived passengers had as many suitcases as the older lady who now entered the door, puffing and swearing.

The lady had obvious problems keeping the white-lacquered metal door open. When it was her turn the automatic door opener had given up for good. This was not her day, so to speak.

She entered, but with the outmost effort; it didn't go smoothly at all. The lady was dressed in a Stetson hat, blue jeans and a jacket in the same material. As a complement to this she was wearing glasses with frames in yellow metal, it might even be gold. It was all very intense. She wasn't a day under seventy-five. Suddenly it was nothing weird about that, everyone has the right to wear any kind of glasses they want, but she would have been more in level with her status as a senior citizen without those frames. She had bought them, she was wearing them, and it wasn't much harder than that.

"What's happening now?" she asked straight into the air in front of her with a cracked, tired and hoarse voice.

Her voice was like coming from a distance very far away, it was hard to grasp that it came from that old lady. She was in a manner of speaking not really in the proper end of that voice.

No one answered. Everybody just stared at her, like she was a woman from Mars. The lady didn't seem to bother about being in the center of things, but it didn't help much either. She was standing in the blaze of gazes and it was only one way out.

The lady took action, went up to the ticket teller and asked:

"When does the next bus for Las Vegas leave?"

She gave the young man behind the ticket desk a demanding gaze. She was expecting him to answer. She looked like she was used to being obeyed.

At least she had that gaze; a gaze that won't take any nonsense, but indicates that everybody in front of her is standing there in order to help her.

The young man behind the counter quickly looked up and looked at her in a moment's silence. That young man suddenly became very tired. His job was really wearing him down.

The young man had a sudden flashback to his early teens, they stood out so brutally against the background of this lady. He had never experienced anything like this.

Then the ticket guy, without commenting, brought out the timetable and studied it very thoroughly. It was not possible to decide whether he was looking for the next bus to Las Vegas or if he was trying to learn the timetable by heart.

Maybe it didn't make any difference whatever he did, he created the time he needed to come up with something to tell the old lady. It took some time. It was like the young man was struggling with much more than just time and something to say to the lady in the Stetson hat.

The young man looked very unhappy there for a moment. He didn't just make that unhappy face that is reserved for a very young person who has no real reason to look unhappy.

That miserable face of his was serious; it was deeply rooted within him. Existing deep down in the root of his heart.

"Half past four tomorrow, p.m." said the young man finally and shut the timetable.

He did it with the slickness that only the very newly employed are capable of. He was standing very calm and smiled at the lady, like he was waiting for something.

The old lady didn't seem to be convinced, she looked at him with her flint hard eyes, taking her time. She wasn't going to give up easily, that was crystal clear.

"Alright. Can I wait here until then?" she asked and gazed at the ticket vendor with eyes, reinforced by her golden glasses.

It seemed like she was trying to look right through him, but she stopped before she even got half way.

"No, we're closing at one o'clock tonight, in about half an hour." the young man replied rapidly, like he most of all wanted her to leave right away, long before the depot closed. Or at least before she started to trouble him for real.

"Can't you arrange a bus for me right now?" the old lady asked.

She was still holding on to her suitcases. They were attached to her wrinkled hands, but she was in style, hadn't yet put them down on the floor. Apparently she was a strong lady. She wasn't about giving up right away. Was probably set on getting where she was going, wherever that was.

"Ma'm, we run our business according to our schedule! We can't get you a bus when you feel for a ride." The young man answered, still very polite.

You could sense that he was making an effort to be very forthcoming. He had not yet become blunted enough to be snotty.

"Whatever am I going to do until tomorrow afternoon?" She threw her question right out into the air, like she was waiting for suggestions from the young man, or from the other passengers. No one answered her. A unanimous silence filled the waiting area, like everyone present had agreed not to help her.

"Do you have a telephone here?" she asked the young man and took a quick glance around the waiting area, like she wanted to discover if he was hiding a phone from her.

The young man did just that. He simply took a look around like he was checking that all the passengers and the locals were his witnesses that he helped the old lady without complaining. Giving sturdy help way beyond the requirements of his employment with the bus company. Help that he, out of goodness, directed specifically towards the elderly lady and all helpless people in general. He was willing to give that help, especially when other people watched him doing it.

"There's a pay phone over there!" the young man said and nodded towards a spot somewhere behind the old lady.

She turned and pulled out a small black notebook. The she walked with somewhat weary steps towards the two pay-phones beside the lockers. She choose one of the phones and looked frenetically for a phone number in her book.

It seemed at the same time like she couldn't really make up her mind to phone, or not. Maybe she had difficulties reading her notes in the sparse yellow light in the bus depot. She halted for a long while and leafed through her notebook before stepping up to one of the pay phones.

"Don't use that one, ma'm! Use the one to the left, it works. The other one will just take your money." A man commented from a bench. He chuckled, like he had said something funny.

"This one?" She nodded towards one of the pay phones.

"Exactly!"

The man on the bench leaned back and for a moment it looked like he was going to raise his arms above his head, but he changed his mind in the last second, like he was on to something. He looked around the premises with a fast, hunted gaze.

The old lady called the operator and asked for a number. She silently held the phone against her ear. She had to adjust the Stetson in order to make room for the phone, but she didn't take off the hat.

"Nah, I want a collect call." she said. "My name is Agnes Buff and I really want to speak to my granddaughter.

There was some seconds of silence.

"Hi, Nancy, is that you? I'm planning to come over tomorrow. Your mum said it probably was going to be okay."

"Well, I'm in the bus depot in … what's the name of this city?" She asked straight out into the waiting area.

The old lady, or Agnes Buff as we now know was her name, sent an interrogative gaze at the other people waiting. No one seemed to feel the urge to respond, that was clear. It was some time before the guys in the waiting area reacted.

"Rapid City, South Dakota," someone answered.

Agnes Buff repeated the location into the phone. She did it with a precision and too much clearness that indicated that her granddaughter wasn't that bright, maybe was three years old, or something like that.

"Yeah, hold on … Nah, I don't know. Hold on a moment and I'll ask the ticket guy if he knows."

But when the old lady turned around the ticket guy was busy with some new travellers.

"Yeah, I know it's long distance! I'll … okay I'd better call you tomorrow," Agnes Buff said, hung up the phone and returned to the ticket counter.

She waited for a couple of minutes while other passengers got their tickets and some answers to their questions. But it wasn't in a positive mood she stood there waiting.

She showed her irritation tapping her fingers with the golden rings on the counter.

"Where am I supposed to spend the night?" She asked when the other travellers had gone.

Agnes Buff was clearly expecting the young man behind the counter to solve her problem, that was totally clear.

"Would you like to find a hotel room, ma'm?" The young man asked, "there's one nearby, just a block to walk."

"How much do they charge here?" Agnes Buff wondered and her voice made it clear that she hadn't really expected this. She looked very tired. Like her age suddenly had overcome her.

"I'm not sure", the young man answered, "but I think they charge like fourteen dollars".

It sounded like he himself had spent a night or two at that motel. He blushed somewhat; you might think that it had to do with some kind of amorous escapade he didn't like the rest of the city's citizens among the people in the waiting area to find out much more about.

"Expensive," Agnes Buff said.

She shook her head, like it was the poor ticket vendors fault, but the people waiting and watching were rooting for the ticket vendor.

They hoped she wasn't getting at him. They stared at Agnes Buff. A bit mean, if you want to interpret it like that.

"If you like you can probably spend the night at the police station," the young man said.

At first it seemed like Agnes Buff couldn't believe her ears. Did the nice young man behind the counter think she was that cheap? Now she could not sleep in the bus depot like she had began planning to do when she realised she wouldn't go directly to Las Vegas, like she had thought.

"Young man, where did you say the motel was?" Agnes Buff asked, because now she had almost made up her mind.

Maybe it took something more serious than a far too young ticket vendor to change the mind of the old lady.

"To the left as you go out the door, only half a block to walk," the young man answered.

"Thanks," Agnes Buff said.

She began walking towards the door with all her suitcases bumping at her legs. It was a sad sight. Agnes Buff looked old and worn. She took the wrong door; attempting to enter the restroom with all her suitcases. Nobody commented; everyone in the waiting area sat in silence and watched her fighting her suitcases.

"What door?"

She asked in a low voice.

But she was not giving up; she was determined to enter that restroom door even though her suitcases occupied her hands and she wasn't going to be able to enter that door with all the suitcases in her hands.

"What's going on?"

The ticket vendor asked and leaned forward over the counter. He had had his mind elsewhere; that was clear and understandable.

"The white door, ma'm," a man in a blue baseball cap said and lit a new cigarette on the stub of the old one he had just been puffing on.

He did that with the automatic movement of a person who has been smoking for so long that this pattern of movement has replaced all others. He didn't know anymore how not to lite a new cigarette on the one you're just about to put out.

Agnes Buff found the right door, but couldn't turn the door knob with suitcases in both hands. She put some down on the floor. Eventually she managed to escape out into the darkness.

Everybody in the waiting area smiled. She was tough lady in spite of her seemingly erratic behavior.

Some on the waiting crowd lit cigarettes, others kept on reading books or magazines. The ticket vendor leaned over the counter and asked the man in the blue baseball cap:

"How is it working out?"

The ticket vendor leaned over even further and supported himself on his elbows.

"I kind of talked to her, but I'd rather not tell what she said." The man in the blue baseball cap said and made a waving gesture with his hands.

"So, you'll be travelling again?"

The ticket vendor said, kind of accusative.

No one else in the waiting area interfered with the conversation between the two men. Maybe someone had the urge to do it, but at the same time it was a very private conversation, even if it took place in a public place.

"Yeah, but as I said, I'd rather not talk about it."

*

The man in the blue baseball cap looked down into the floor like there really was something very interesting to watch there. There wasn't, that was clear to everyone else in the waiting area.

Finally the man in the blue cap realized that too. It just took him a bit longer than the rest of the people in the waiting area.

"That bad, eh?"

The ticker vendor said in a soothing voice. He seemed very interested in that phone call and its consequences. Maybe it was just like it appeared, but he looked interested.

"Yeah," muttered the guy in the blue cap.

He moved a bit uneasy on the bench. It seemed like he wanted the young man behind the counter to stop talking about it, whatever they were talking about.

At the same time he just didn't want to tell the young man in a harsh manner that he didn't want to talk about it. It was like he wanted it both ways. Like the man in the blue baseball cap both wanted to talk about it and at the same time, not.

"Tough luck," said the young ticket vendor, looking seriously at the man in the blue baseball cap and getting wrinkles on his forehead. He was really feeling sympathetic for the man in the blue baseball cap and that was more than any of the others in the waiting area had come up with.

"You could say that again!" the man in the blue cap sighed.

Now he was appearing happier and seemed to have left the idea of studying the floor. The guy behind the counter liked that. It was more fun to be able to see the eyes of the one you were talking to, then they had more contact and exchange of comments. Like the whole thing wasn't more than a game, like the fact that something was happening wasn't that important. Maybe this was the wrong place, at the completely wrong point in time; but it seemed like they were attempting at closing some kind of peace in the waiting area. The big, still remaining, question was if they had ever been at war. They smiled at each other. The man in the blue baseball cap produced a somewhat tense smile; but the ticker vendor seemed to be only curious, in spite of his constant smiling.

He had that kind of face, looking like a weasel, but it was somewhat taken down by his smile: and that was his luck. It had been too awful if that sneaky trait had been the main one.

It would appear that they had a lot of things in common, but it hadn't to. It could be about shear and clear politeness too. It was too hard to decide how close the two men were. It's always like that. Them talking to each other didn't necessarily mean that they knew each other. They could have met just twenty minutes ago.

Or maybe they had grown up together in a back yard somewhere forty years ago and never been separated more than two-three days at a time.

It is always hard to decide how such things really are. You just cannot see it on people.

When the door to the bus depot was closed it was easy to forget that it was late at night and it was really dark outside.

Inside the sparingly lit building a part of the day was still lingering. There was some activity going on; and activity was probably lacking out there in the streets.

There was a lonely neon light shining in through a window, but it was to up to debate if there was something out there. Rapid City, South Dakota, is not a town that is steaming with life and action. Even if it was a Friday night it was as calm as ever. Calm and dark. Friday night may not be a typical night to take the temperature on an unknown town, but if it was, it may be decisive. If you compare nights in different towns it would be the base for comparison.

The white lacquered door was swung ajar and Agnes Buff entered again. All the gazes of the crowd were drawn towards the door. Agnes Buff's eyes looked way more tired this time. Now she had been out there in the darkness with all them suitcases for a while. They had taken their toll on her; that was starting to show now. Some more trouble and that jeans-clad old lady would really soften and yield to the cold reality of Friday night.

"Where did he say that the motel was? I can't find it," Agnes Buff said with a measure of despair in her voice.

She really didn't want it to show, so she was still using a hard, aggressive voice, like she probably had done all life long. Maybe she happened to give the wrong impression, but that was hard to tell when you'd only met her briefly in a bus depot.

"Half a block up on the left side," the man in the blue baseball cap answered.

It was just like he avoided looking at her, even though he had spoken to her a couple of times. He was the person in the waiting area who had spoken to Agnes Buff most times since she appeared.

"I can't find it! Do they have a sign outside?" Agnes Buff asked.

It appeared that it was not working out so well for her. She wanted help; that was clear to everyone in the waiting area. No one could misjudge that.

"Yes, it says 'Motel 400' on large signs." The guy in the blue baseball cap said, "half a block; you can't miss it, ma'm!"

The man in the baseball cap appeared tired of the old lady; it was like she couldn't make up her mind to leave the bus depot; and that was certainly odd. There was not that much that could attract people to it, really.

Some nights are like that. They end before they start, like they had been too short from the beginning. That's how weird some nights become.

There's something definitely wierd about the depots of the Greyhound lines. They are life scaled down into a miniature. They are the heart of the countryside's contacts with the rest of the world.

The passengers had left their buses to enter the depot, but Agnes Buff had come in from her bus and now, from the street.

There is something absolutely terrifying about waiting areas. It's the way it is in the constant waiting areas we pass between birth and death. Some buses and trains, coming in, is not the kind of winners we first assumed they were. For some passengers the waiting area is just a change of transportation, for others an adventure to pass it. It all depends on who you happen to be, and when you happen to be in the waiting area.

The presence in the waiting area can seem like an eternity and it may be like a bat of an eye, all that depending on the moment.

There's nothing mandatory about waiting areas. They are there and it's possible to use them, but it's also possible to avoid them. You decide for yourself.

You have already made the decision to be in the waiting area once you've entered it. It's all your own decisions combined that decide what you get out of that visit to the waiting area. Some times you get the impression that you don't have the option to decide, but that is often just a feeling of discomfort. The discomfort isn't there.

"Thanks," Agnes Buff said and disappeared out into the darkness again. This time nobody smiled. There was nothing to smile at any more. It had started to get boring. Nobody wanted to see Agnes Buff return one more time, and no one cared if she found that motel or not.

They had stopped smiling; it was that kind of night.

You're looking at the next president

They say a lot of stupid stuff on television. What is said on television is in that regard no way different from what is said in regular life. The difference is just that through the TV that crap is distributed to a whole lot of people. Then some people will discover that it is just a lot of crap, and some won't.

The glimmer from the TV-set is filling the shady room. The bluish flickering light breaks up the lines of the room. No stable points are left. The barren walls become vibrant in the flickering, blue-white light. The blue jacket of corduroy, slung over the chair in the middle of the room takes the shape of a sitting person.

It creates a pair with the man in the wide bed in front of the TV-set. His body is creating a wary flickering shadow on the wall. Like that shadow has a life of its own.

The nighttime is the part of the day when people with a good conscience are sleeping. It is also when people with good consciences in general assume that people with a bad conscience are wide awake.

The ones who are worried by the thought that there are people with bad consciences are awake too and are thinking about how they will avoid being struck by chronically bad consciences. The night is the time when everything bad in our lives surfaces from being hidden and teases and irritates, maybe because you have more time for undisturbed thinking.

The night follows certain rules, like everything else in life, but the night has its own logic, its own mystic. The night turns life upside down, changes the ordinary and boringly everyday run of the mill into something that at least to some degree looks like the life we all are dreaming about, or into something we are dreaming.

This is the life when we overtake all them daydreams, the distant goals of our longing, when they become real and we don't have to yearn for them anymore.

But the night is also the time when everything ordinary becomes really strange and frightening, when we see shadows in what earlier has been sunlit and inviting.

In all that lies a challenge, but everyone doesn't like that kind of challenge. There is fear that freezes our lost souls out there in the darkness. The ice weighs us down until we don't know what we are doing.

"Draw!" The man in front of the TV says and points with his index finger at the flickering image.

He smiles a bit and lowers his hand, with his index finger still erect.

It takes time to get used to that things happen in a certain manner. When we have gotten used to it we have difficulties accepting that things are happening suddenly in a different way than what we are used to.

The night shows us the shadows of our lives, the things we'd rather forget that we carry, but they are there, buried deep inside us. The things we cannot escape from.

Of course all the shadows have their own life. They are not totally separated from the things they are the shadows of. But they live a reasonably free life, not influenced by things that is happening to their hosts.

Maybe the shadow really is there, all on its own. It wouldn't surprise the owner of the shadow. He has stopped letting himself get surprised, it was a long time ago since he thought anything was strange. He doesn't want to be impressed by stuff that only seems to happen around him.

He's not even sure what he's doing anymore. It might be the other way around. He can't separate what is different from what is not. Maybe that's not the most important thing he can occupy himself with right now. Way too many things fill his brain at the moment; way too much seems important.

The man on the bed is holding a revolver in his hand, a Colt of a model that was common in the army in the 19th century. Then Colts mills in Connecticut succeeded in making weapons with totally interchangeable parts, which resulted in a prosperous spare-part business. Of course it was the corner stone of an exceptionally profitable weapons industry, the old gunsmiths almost immediately fell out of fashion.

The man on the bed often feels out of fashion in a manner that is hard to pin down.

He doesn't really know what to make out of that feeling. If he would get around doing anything it would

Vandelier's Song

probably be about getting away from the flickering light in this room.

The way things have developed lately there's nothing pushing him to go anywhere. He's stuck in this room, stuck in a way he just a few years ago couldn't have imagined even in his wildest dreams.

Three empty cans of Coors and a half empty bottle of whiskey are standing in front of the man on the low table between the bed and the table where the TV-set is sitting.

The man's face is fuzzy in the faint light from the TV screen. Only his dark eyes seem clearly visible. Maybe it's more eye-sockets than eyes in the common sense. They are dark as abysses.

His face seems pale and worn. When the man on the bed takes aim with the Colt he shuts one eye. He's face becomes distorted and his mouth disfigured. He lives in the center of his game with the heavy revolver. He exists only when he holds the smooth metal in his hand. Anything else is impossible.

He has stopped functioning when he can't feel the metal against his skin, or maybe he has discovered that he's only like he wants to be when he is holding the revolver. He doesn't know for sure and it's nothing that worries him neither.

There is a knock on the door and he flinches.

Then he moves very fast and shuts the TV-set off. When he approaches the door he's holding the Colt behind his back.

The barrel close to his spine, his wrist twisted in an

awkward angle. It's like he most of all wants to get rid of that hand, like he don't want to keep it. He stalls answering the door; don't want to be too fast again. That has gone wrong earlier and might do that again. He doesn't want to take that risk.

The last weeks he has felt threatened. He doesn't know by what, or by whom, has just had that vague feeling that someone is watching him. He hasn't really seen anything, but is still sure that somebody is keeping an eye on him. It doesn't matter whom.

"Howdy Cliff," there's a voice from the other side of the door.

The man stiffens a bit, not much, but he's showing kind of hesitation that doesn't go along with the revolver. He knows that voice, it's coming from somewhere in his past. There are a lot of other voices in his past, but this one he remembers very well.

"Hi Helen," Cliff then mumbles after a brief moment's hesitation.

He tucks the revolver inside his belt so the barrel rests in the crack between his buttocks. The metal feels chilly.

Cliff straightens in his efforts to avoid contact with the metal, but at the same time it's kind of comforting. He can't make up his mind how he is going to have it with that barrel. He opens the door and lets the woman whose voice he remembers from his past, inside.

"I was on my way home from the cabin. Thought you should offer me something to drink", Helen says.

She looks at Cliff. She is a rather short woman in her 30-ties.

"Okay, come in," Cliff mumbles.

Cliff backs a few steps into the room, but is still blocking the doorway. Like he doesn't really wants to let the woman inside.

Maybe he feels threatened by her, somehow she sends signals to him that he doesn't understand. That kind of guesswork he wants to avoid.

"I'm not bothering you, am I?" Helen asks and is hesitating in the doorway.

Maybe she wants him to let her pass, maybe she thinks they're standing to close.

"Nah, I was only watching TV," Cliff says, "what will it be?"

Cliff studies her, looking for something more. It's not impossible that she wants more than just a drink, even if he doesn't understand what that could be.

"A squirt of whiskey with a lot of soda", says Helen after a glance at the bottle on the table.

She steps into the room with sudden self-esteem, as if it blossoms as she enters the room, as if she is filled with it only when she is in the room.

Helen fills her part of the room in the obvious way, that only the one who never had been forced to hide is capable of.

Cliff asks himself why he doesn't have the same way to exist, the same manner to move about in a room. The question may be superfluous, he knows very well why. He does not need to ask, not even himself.

"Whiskey I have, but no soda," Cliff mutters and takes the opportunity to put his revolver in the bread can on the bench in the kitchen when he fetches some ice.

While in the kitchen he looks around there, like to check that everything is the same as the last time he was there. Like to check that nothing is out of place that should not be.

When he gets into the room again, Helen has slammed down on the couch. She leafs through an old issue of Newsweek and seems distraught. There's nothing new to her, since he can remember she always has had her times of absence. Sure, she's there, but she's not in, as they say.

"So, you've been in the back country?"

He asks in passing, like he doesn't want to get involved in the conversation.

"Yeah, I saw my sister in New Haven," says Helen.

She looks at him, somewhat hesitantly. It seems like she doesn't feel safe around him, like she's ill at ease in his company.

Maybe that's the way it has always been between them, he doesn't really remember how it was in the old days. It seems so long ago now. Time has put an eternity between what was and what is.

"Beth?" he wonders, halfheartedly, like he is grasping for a well known name in a river of completely unknown occurrences.

He still remembers some stuff, it's not that. But most of the time so many new things and emotions threaten to drown him every day. He can't stand up to them any more.

"Right, you've met her!"

She looks pensively at him for a long time and the she asks:

"How are things really with you? Is everything okay?"

Helen smiles at him and tilts her head in that manner that always made her get away with anything, in the old days. Now it doesn't work that way anymore, but he notices it and that's at least something.

Cliff shrugs and sits down on the floor in front of the bed. He puts the glass of whiskey and ice beside him. He fumbles with a pack of cigarettes.

"Well, I guess that's the same old, same old," he says, with no real conviction.

He doesn't seem especially alert, but not on his way to fall asleep either, just a bit worn down. Out of shape to put it straight up.

"Any work yet?" she asks.

Helen puts her question in a tone like it might be the most obvious thing in the world if he hadn't gotten any job, like she doesn't care a bit how things are working out for him.

"Right, I parked cars at a place in the neighborhood for a while. But I don't know … Got so nervous doing that, so I quit. I have some dollars left though, I'm gonna look for something next week or so …"

"You're not gonna continue with the proofreading?" she asks, looking at him, like she's waiting for his reaction.

"I wasn't a proofreader! I edited articles!" snaps Cliff.

He puffs heavily on his cigarette and then stumps it out in an already overfull ashtray on the low table.

"Oh, sorry! I did know that, but to me they are almost the same," Helen mumbles a bit absent minded.

It's like she's not listening to what he is saying, at least he gets that impression. And the feeling it has in tow is also a familiar one, he's had it for many years now, he doesn't seem to get totally rid of it.

"Not to me, but okay. Lets not talk any more about it," Cliff mumbles.

He takes a swig out of the whiskey. He swallows rapidly, without really tasting it. He's surprised that he cares so much about what Helen calls the job he once had. He has problems recognising himself.

To be honest he really doesn't recognise Helen's behavior either.

They are quiet for a while. They taste the silence spreading out between them. They have some gulps from their glasses and kind of avoid looking at each other.

"Do you have any girlfriend?" Helen asks abruptly.

Cliff makes a long look at her. He picks out a new cigarette and lights it clumsily. He wonders if he wants to answer that question, but makes up his mind to go to no trouble. Why does he make a fuzz about answering?

"Haven't had any ambitions in that area since you left with that lawyer or whatever he was," he says without looking at her, like he doesn't want her to see his eyes, like he's avoiding something.

Maybe it's not that way at all, but you never know, do you? Maybe it's just a bad habit, a manner of moving he has found out worked for him some time and then has incorporated in his pattern of movements. Or, maybe it's something completely different.

"He's no lawyer. But that doesn't matter. Don't you see any people at all then?" she wonders and tilts her head.

"Some, at work and stuff like that," Cliff states vaguely.

He wonders what she's after. He doesn't really understand her questions. Cliff doesn't understand what is interesting about him. He doesn't get what she's after; if she's after anything at all. He can't decide.

"You must get out and meet people. You can't hide here and grieve for the rest of your life," she says.

He jolts, it really sounds like she is meaning what she's saying. He finds that peculiar. It really has been a long time since he traced something like that in her voice. It surprises him a lot.

"Alright, I'm gonna do that," Cliff says .

But there's no real conviction in his voice. It's like the air has gone out of him. He doesn't seem to have any sparkle left in him. Maybe he has given up, but it is not entirely clear that it is in that way.

"What?" Helen wonders.

Like if she hasn't listened, even though she's been in the room all of the time, at the same time as Cliff.

He gets a bit irritated over that. Not much, but just enough to become a bit mad.

"Meeting people," he says.

He gets disturbed by the fact that she doesn't seem to keep track of what he's saying. It was like that in the old days too. It's nothing new she has picked up along the way, he knows that all to well.

"Okay! I'd better be on my way, it's an early morning coming up," she says.

It sounds like a bad excuse to leave in a hurry. But Cliff makes no comment, just accepting that she's getting away without really visiting him. Maybe he doesn't even care that much anymore. Maybe she is part of the past now. Maybe it's over. Maybe her influence and power over him has vanished. He doesn't really believe it.

"Right. Okay. Thanks for stopping by," Cliff says in a low voice.

He just wants her to leave and stay at the same time. He doesn't get why he is so ambivalent about her when he meets Helen.

She's nice, but it feels like she's cut a piece off him, deep down inside. Maybe not willingly, but there's something there anyway. It's there and makes the chatting with her become a mixture of despair and hope from his point of view in any case.

"Should've stopped bye earlier, but … Yeah, you know …"

Helen's voice fades away like she doesn't know what to say. It seems strange when happening to her. It doesn't suit her at all.

They walk towards the door. Helen opens the door

and Cliff holds the door open for her while she's exiting. It's like they have done that so many times that it has grown into a habit, no, a bad habit, to act like that.

There are all too many things you do in that unreflective manner, brushing your teeth, going to the bathroom, holding up door and watch out at the red lights.

Cliff wonders what kind of gigantic conspiracy lies behind all that. You would think that there's some kind of objective purpose with all them absurdities you are taught all life long.

"Hey you?" he says.

It's not his intention to sound weak, but he feels he's doing it anyway. He has no choice when he faces her. She has that impact on him. It's depressing, but it's the way it is, or he just blames himself since he does not know what he wants.

"Yes. What is it?" she asks, judiciously, he thinks. But he is not sure she is tampering with him. It may be an entirely natural voice mode she has. Cliff does not really recognise it. He thinks he should know all her voices. It only shows how little he really knows about Helen.

"I am just wondering. Are you still hanging out with that guy?" he says, looking at her as if he does not dare to see her straight in the face.

He is surprised at his own behavior, but it's not the first time it happens. He has been in this situation several times before.

"Ted, you mean?" she says and squints towards him

through the dense tobacco smoke, which fills out the bright parts of the TV-set's flickering light cascades.

The room seems to vibrate, but he knows it's only that strange light from the TV that interferes with the usual contours of the room.

"Yes," he responds, more abruptly than he initially intended.

She has a strange impact on him. For some reason she has always had that. Cliff has never understood what is causing him to be influenced by her in that strange way. He only gets confused when he thinks about it.

There is nothing he wants to think about.

"No, we have not met for a three to four months," she says, looking him straight into the eyes.

It's as though she's proving something to him. Like she thinks it's important for him to know how it is.

He does not understand why.

"Oh," Cliff mumbles.

He is wondering why he even bothered to ask. He doesn't know what he should do about Helen's answer. As if she'd been wrong answering him. She would never have been able to say something that made him happy.

"Bye!" Helen says.

Helen leaves without turning around once. Cliff wonders if they will ever see each other again. Helen does not seem particularly keen. Maybe he himself is not too keen to resume the old relationship. Perhaps it is impossible; he repents not asking.

Vandelier's Song

"Bye!" Cliff mumbles when he closes the door after her.

It definitely seems that in some way he doesn't understand what he is doing. He sits on the couch and turns on the sound on the television. Sitting there in the fluttering light. There is something very restful and definite about the flickering pictures on the sharp-edged box, something in there that are no other place in life, something better than life itself. After a minute he stands up, walks into the kitchen and returns with the Colt in his hand. He settles down and continue looking at the TV-show. It's a long inter-view with the president. Cliff hears the president talking about energy crisis and raised petrol prices.

The president looks worried and Cliff does not like that. He does not like people who look worried. There is something very wrong with such people. He has never gotten used to watching them. He wishes they will come to their senses. But they just go on. That president has looked worried for a long time. He looked worried long before he was elected president. It was astonishing that the guy was elected with all the worries of the world already painted on his face.

Cliff does not like it.

He really does not like it, it's a threatening aura lingering around him, just thinking about it. So he'd rather forget about it all. But. It's easy to think about forgetting and another thing to really forget. Cliff does not have enough willpower to know that he does not know when he tries to decide to do something, either one or the other. He rests in the mind of the image of the once cheerful president and does not like how it is now. Not that either. He seems to have ended up in a dead end. He does not like anything about the president, nothing and it makes him even more depressed.

He is tired of being so depressed, but there is not much he can do about it, he simply doesn't have a clue what to do about it. He is very confused and disappointed. Then he lifts the Colt and start pulling the trigger. He shuts his eyes when his index finger pulls the trigger backwards. He must close his eyes, like someone else and not himself, controls that index finger. As if his index finger had taken command of his life, as though his finger controls him now, nothing else.

His index finger lives a very separate life, as if it has become part of his free-flowing shadow, as if it is no longer connected to the rest of him. It is both worrying and liberating, at the same time. He has never understood people who claim that life is about wanting stuff as hard as you can, to be able to cope with everything, when you have knowledge enough.He thinks it's just a sneak peek; things just happen, you don't have a chance in hell to do anything about them.

They are there; all them events, and they throw themselves over you, without doing the very least to control themselves. Everything else is just a sneak peek; he has not been able to influence his own life at all. All he knows with certainty is that his index finger now acts entirely on its own. He cannot control it. He is guided by his index finger.

He feels a violent anxiety attack, has no control over what's happening. Pieces from the TV-set swirl into the room. They spread in the air, as if trying to fill it out as quickly as possible without Cliff being able to do anything about it. The litter flyes around in slow motion in the small room. One of them lands on the chest on Cliff's white T-shirt. It obscures some of the text on his shirt.

The text says: "YOU'RE LOOKING AT THE NEXT PRESIDENT".

The Witch Master of Self-Pity

The room is all too quiet. Craig Davis guesses that's why he wakes up. He sighs. He had hoped to skip this day, but that's obviously not the way it works. He's disappointed.

The bright flower pattern on the quilt wrinkles when Craig Davis moves it aside and with sleep dry eyes looks at the red numbers on the digital clock in the darkness. It's early. The clock shows not more than 06:32.

It's almost half an hour earlier than he's used to wake up. He turns the alarm on the clock off. He has a glimmer of a thought wondering if he saved some electricity not letting the clock chime.

Craig isn't really a guy who thinks about saving, but thought like that whirls through his head of most people, he thinks.

He's a regular guy, has no motivation to save on stuff. That's at least the way it has been until now. Now the situation has changed a bit. That's what he has trouble adjusting to.

Since it's early there's not much about Craig Davis either, as a manner of speaking. Rising early in the morning has never been his cup of tea. It hasn't become easier as the years have passed either, not like people use to insist.

There seems to be some kind of flagellation attitude driven to pure art. And like all forms of art even this has it dedicated supporters.

Craig has never understood people who step out of bed in the morning with a song on their lips. He has never belonged to them and now there's even less of a reason to rise with a song.

The singing and dancing has in a way run out of his life and he doesn't need to rise early to understand that. It feels the same way even if he rises at lunch time, at the earliest, he knows that for sure.

He has gone through periods when he was thinking it was important to rise early, but has never really gotten used to that.

Craig isn't totally sure he could have gotten used to early rising. Now he is looking upon it like it isn't worth the effort to rise at all. Now it's really an effort even to think about it.

He is trying to avoid thinking about that resistance. In a way it's not the resistance that's interesting, but the morning that lies in front of him like an unbaked roll of bread.

Craig pulls the shades open with a rather sudden movement and looks through the dirty windowpane. It's raining there on the other side of the glass. In the pale light of morning a haze of rain covers the roofs with a grey filter. He sees that the No Name restaurant hasn't opened yet.

At least it's not coming any light from the windows out of them unto the street, but you can never be completely sure. He has been surprised earlier. So why not now? But he is trying to be sincere, he is not particularly interested in any surprises. Recently, life has been very full of the likes. Sufficient for several years to come. He certainly does not know why he's even going upstairs. It's harder than he had imagined possible. It's like all his strength ran out of him, as though he pressed the last drop out of his willpower, as if there is nothing more left to drive him forward. It makes him feel low at heart, but it does not matter, a bit more depression makes no difference, it has already spilled over. Perhaps there is only an allotted portion of energy for every human being.

When it wears out, you are seriously speaking about beginning to die, Craig thinks. Not because No-Name was a place where he would like to have breakfast, it was too expensive for that. But he liked to consider the crowds of people outside the pub in the evenings. It was fun to compare the different speeds of the different days. Of course he is thinking about the intensity of the crowds during different parts of the day. He thinks he can read it by noticing how many persons come and go around No-Name. Especially right outside of No-Name. It's as though that restaurant would be special in some way. Perhaps because he has watched it so many times; both from the window and when he passed by it. He has also had meals at No-Name, but he does not really remember what he had to eat or how it tasted like. It might say more about the quality of the place than about Craig's memory. To that end, he has reason to doubt it now. His failing memory is now resulting in that in two weeks time he will have trouble keeping the car, the apartment and all the other stuff he has acquired in recent years. Then he probably will get no salary anymore. Then his possibilities to live as he has done so far will end abruptly. And he only has himself to blame. He had the chance to gather some "fuck off capital", but he did not take it. It will probably never happen again. He can not imagine he's going to reboot.

It is always as fascinating to consider food-joints. It is as though people are rallying around them in a particular way; as if there is a special attraction in those restaurants. Obviously, the food may attract people, maybe the liquor too, but Craig often thinks you generally are sitting down waiting more than you eat at such places.

So it's inefficient, especially if you are stressed and would like to sit down and work instead of having to spend half an hour waiting for the food. Now he has no longer any general objection to restaurants, now he has all the time in the world. But now he cannot afford to go to restaurants as often as before. He feels strangely stressed that he will have so much time at his disposal in the future. He does not know how to behave.

Craig walks into the bathroom and turns on the water heater. He steps in under the shower allowing the water to wake him out of his semi-detached state. Nobody likes Craig Davis. Yes, there is one. Craig Davis himself, but it does not count. In any case, there is no newcomer to the mourning. If there is something he is good at, it's feeling sorry for himself. He is a witch master of self-pity. There seems to be nothing he likes, and for as long as he tends to feel sorry for himself. It has periodically been his most popular hobby. One problem with such a hobby is that it is not particularly inspiring. It's not a good idea to keep on pitying yourself. It is destructive. He is wondering if he will bounce back in a few days, or in a few weeks, when his money will be at its lowest. As he gets out of the shower, it is still raining, he notices through the bathroom window. It's a calm rain. He is grateful for it being there.

This raining increases the humidity in the air. He has trouble if it gets too dry. At least in the mornings. Then it appears that a little more moisture prevents the tendency of his throat to recoil.

He experienced some terrible autumns when he was a child, could not get air and lay gasping for his breath until the doctor came and said that he did not tolerate the air. But what could his parents do about it? They did not have any money to let him go somewhere where he would feel better. He got better when he grew up. But he never forgets how hard it was to breathe, how excited he felt when they got him to sit up and breathe and at the same time thought that they were holding him too hard so that he could not breathe. It was as though his mother and father forced the air out of him.

Afterwards he realized that it was not like that, but the memories are not fooled, they force themselves on his statements. He wears a pair of black chinos and a light blue shirt. In the kitchen he looks into the fridge. That is no uplifting sight. Half of the cabinet is filled with beer cans. The other half is empty. There is also a can of light mayonnaise. Craig sighs when he closes the fridge door. He goes out into the hall. When the phone rings, he just has to stretch out his hand and easily reach the handset.

"Hi, Craig, it's Mom!"

It is as if she's disappearing further away from everyday life every year. Like she's driving somewhere where no one else can follow her. Sometimes he gets worried over it. But he never says anything to her about it, that would not make any difference. She would only be annoyed with him.

"I hear that, mom!"

He is filled with some kind of hopelessness when she calls. As if her telephone conversation constantly brakes him down a bit, as if she wants to subdue him before he starts the day at too high a pace. He does not know if it's true, or if it's just like he imagines.

"I just wanted to remind you that you and John promised to have dinner with me tomorrow," she says.

"I have not forgotten!"

His voice sounds weak when he speaks.

"Can you remember to drive past Herzenberg's bakery and get some bread?" she asks. "I'll call them and order what you should pick up, so you don't have to do anything more than get it?"

"Is it down by Bloomingdale's?"

It's as if he is stuck with playing a child over and over his entire life, he never escapes that old role she gave him. He wonders if it is like that for other people too, or if he is completely alone in terms of that role playing as well.

"Yes, just around the corner there!"

He likes to trace the usual annoyance that his lack of grace plants in her voice, but he may miss out on it. It would not be the first time in that case.

"Okay, I'll pick it up my way."

He wants to finish this conversation now. He has an unpleasant feeling that his mother is always ready and able to spend the whole day on the phone unless you stop her. It's as though she still believes she's entitled to all his time.

"Well, then we'll see each other tomorrow."

Craig hangs up and momentarily pity his mother. She is sitting all alone there in that big house. But on the other hand, she has a fair amount of money.

Money brings no direct advantage; she doesn't have to think about money every day, which is a blessing in itself, quite apart from what you can buy for that money. So money is good for those who have it, it facilitates. That's the last thing you need to tell me, he thinks.

Somewhat bitter, he knows everything, but there's just not much to do about it. Not any more. Craig looks at himself in the rear mirror and it makes him possibly more depressed. He is wondering if he is seriously falling through if he is running out of order. He can not really figure out what it's like and he's stumbling on his own mirror image. He sighs, it seems to be the most constructive thing he can imagine. He picks out his jacket out of the closet and leaves the apartment. When he comes down to the garage, he thinks for a moment that it's raining.

He is sitting in his car. He pities himself. Even more pitying himself just since it's raining too. Craig drives slowly out of the garage. It takes guts if you want to get out in that rain.

But there is so much that misfires for Craig Davis right now, it's simply the only thing it does, misfiring. Life has become like a single long ascent, though he thinks he has come to an end, it's strange.It may not matter, because at the moment it seems that everything should be received. Nothing is easy anymore, there are no simple answers and no simple solutions.

Craig is feeling really lonely for maybe the first time in his life. It's a very scary experience. He cannot handle it. He wants to flee, but has nowhere to go. He comes from a very distant point of existence, but has no goal anymore. He drives in the direction of Golden Gate Park. He plans to have an omelet at Cliff House. But he abandons the idea of that and heads into the park by the archery course. Of course there are no archers who practice there in this rain. He is watching the rain falling over the trees in the park.

A woman in red raincoat and white long trousers comes walking through the park with a Golden Retriever. Craig observes the woman outside in the pouring rain. He can not see the woman's face, but her pace and the way she moves makes him think it's a younger woman. Craig does not even know why he cares about thinking that there is a woman out there in the rain. He should think of other things. Not even random women wandering around all alone in the rain.

Craig opens the glove compartment and picks out the revolver located there. He is studying it carefully. The windshields on the car are streaky with the rainwater flowing down from the car roof. The revolver feels cold and hard in his hand. He is fighting an impulse to aim at the woman in the red raincoat, who is exercising her dog in the rainy park. It's tempting to aim at her. His index finger hugs the trigger, but something stops him. It is not his conviction that it is wrong to kill. There is something completely different.

Craig has no real desire to shoot a completely unfamiliar woman. He is more willing to use the revolver on himself. The problem is that he is pitying himself at a level where he does not imagine he can do it. Life has become so absurd that he can not do anything about it, and then it has gone well, he thinks. It's scary that you can slide away in this way, without actually losing your footing, but there's still no way to land at all.

He has come to a situation where he cannot go elsewhere. It hurts not being able to move and it hurts to move. It's really an unsustainable situation and it makes him even more desperate.

He does not recognize his ordinary self in all this. When he thinks back, he realizes that he has never really understood even his most basic needs. He has always postponed everything as if he were to live forever.

Next year I will graduate, then I will … Next month I have more time, then I will… Next week I can meet Joanna, Beth, Susie, or whatever they called, all the missed chances. All the tried and tested opportunities.

All this just because he did not want his circles to blend, just because he wanted to live as close to his schedule as possible. He does not understand what he's been doing. Yes, he knows what he's been doing. But he does not realise that just he fell for that entire myth. It started so well. He had good grades in school all the way. The best thing about it was that he never even had to exert himself.

All those grades were for him, they were waiting for him. He had no problems with that kind of adaptation. When he started to work, however, it always felt weird, but the managers thought he was doing fine and it went well, even though he never liked what he was doing.

The money poured in. It was that kind of business. He thought his colleagues were superficial, but he was not obliged to spend time with them in his spare time. He could live well. But more of his time disappeared to what they called the working life.

Then he felt fooled. And none of all that is a part of the present anymore. There were only memories of a painful time, nothing more. It's like a nightmare, something he has to forget. He is a man who really likes to live a very well-planned, scheduled life. Now that all hours have disappeared overnight, there is nothing that controls him anymore. He disappears, he feels how he is blurred. The old Craig is fading out of the picture, or has already disappeared. He used to be a completely different person. Now he is a new, scary and strange person. It hurts him very much all over. It's as if he lost the old ordinary Craig, which he used to be accustomed to that throughout his life, and got a completely unknown Craig to live with. It does not feel strange.

The rain smears against the roof of the red Mustang. Craig holds the gun in his right hand and lets his index finger on the left hand run along the pipe. The metal is now a bit warmer and now he is not as scared of it anymore. He does not care much about the gun either. It feels more unimportant now than it did during the month that has passed since he bought it. It's as if he got more used to it, as if he now owns it in a different way than when he had just bought it. He sees the woman in the red rain cap disappearing in shelter behind the hay bales at the far end of the archery course. The rain falls as heavily as thoughts.

The park seems to be deserted. Craig feels very lonely. He sees himself as the only person in the park, the only man in the world. It's an abandoning feeling. But, outside the park there are other people. Craig thinks of his mother, gives John a few thoughts too, the brother, whom he will meet tomorrow night. He is not looking forward to the event.

But he simultaneously does not think it's particularly

bad to go there. It will be the same as it always used to be.

A mother's rendezvous with her sons. Predictable and sad, but also homeless and petty in its own manner. The worst thing about their mother is that she does not let John or himself be adults. It's as though she never even considered that concept. He does not know how his mother wants life to be. It's as though she finished living her life from thirty years ago. She can be fine if she wants to, but the worst thing is to hate Craig and John in that past, now a part of history. They live today, while their mother lives in the past. It can never end in more than tears and agony. Craig puts the revolver in the glove compartment, starts the car and drives out of the park. It is still raining, but it seems that it is not a really sustaining rain like just a few minutes ago. On the way to the apartment, he takes the revolver out of the glove compartment and places it next to the passenger seat.

He enters the Golden Gate Bridge and picks up the revolver from the seat. He wants to throw it into the water, but he realises he will not be able to throw it far enough to cross the bridge. He increases the speed, turns down on the road to Sausalito. He throws the revolver on the road.

When he sees the dark metal lump disappearing out of the field of vision, he becomes a little sober. He begins to feel sorry for himself since he has thrown away the revolver instead of selling it and getting some money back for it. He also realises that self-esteem is something he will be stuck without. It is not something that is done in a handful of days, he does not know if he will ever let that self-esteem completely out. It's as if it's totally outside of his power. It is as if he cannot run away a single second from it, as if he is eaten from within by an emotion he cannot identify.

He does not care about the emotions that way, what he now wants is to feel good. He does not want to think much more.

He wants to get a new job and be able to afford to manage his life. He does not want anything more right now. Everything else may come later. Now he has to concentrate on what's important. Nothing else can distract him, he just does not get it. Perhaps there is only an allotted portion of energy for each person. When it disappears, you start to die for real, Craig thinks again.

Someone else can always look at the lives of others and mean they are bad, that people need to take care of their cards better. Craig was such a know-it-all until a few weeks ago. Then he suddenly realised on what fragile grounds he had built his own life. That's when he grasped that you can not be judged by others, especially if you do not live as carefully that you want to celebrate Easter.

When he thinks back on the last few days, he is surprised that he did not shoot at the woman in the park. But in some way, there is still a little bit left in him. However, the race may not be completely lost. It is possible that he can get back on his feet, even if he does

Vandelier's Song

not want to say he hopes for it. Had he shot, everything had been different now. Nothing could have touched him, he would have no need to regret himself or long for Sarah.

It would have been completely different, but there had also been no resort. Now, at least, he has hope there is some sort of continuation. Although it does not look bright.

The car's cooler is still pointing towards Sausalito.

In Sausalito there is Sarah. Craig does not want anything else. But he reminds himself that she lives in Sausalito and not in San Fran. He pities himself because he is sitting alone in the car in the pouring rain.

Drugstore

One of the raindrops that fall must be the first. Of course it is difficult to decide which one. There will be a lot of them falling at once. And it is raining with full force already after a few hesitating seconds. Hopefully the rain cleans the air, but you do not see the sun clear even if it's 99 degrees. The heat makes the skin feel so strained that it just seems to be a matter of time before it falls off the body. But luckily it's raining.

Initially, it's believed that it's a good thing, since you discover that the rain makes no difference. It is the same as before. The only difference is that it's raining. The haze covers the day in a blanket of blurred contours. The air is tacky and the heat clings to the skin. It's as if there's a fear there, a fear that the heat will never end. Perhaps there is reason to believe that it will never end. But with all reasonable faith in the powers of the weather, one must hope for a change.

There is no need to stare at the sky and longing for rain anymore. Now you understand that the rain does not help a bit, it's almost worse when it's raining. It's strange that you can get so stuck on the weather, but if that's what's the most painful, that's why you're so interested in it.

The rain is like a greeting from the cave stage, a greeting from the person we all were very long ago. A whole lot of things have changed, but the rain remains the same. There can be high-raise buildings constructed and traffic routes built around us, electronic toys may occupy more and more of the time we used to call leisure time. But the rain is always the same. The biggest difference is that we do not freeze or get as wet as at the time we lived in caves or earth cabins. That time is not far away, it's there, closer to us than we usually think. We always hope that we will be more comfortable than before. But there is no guarantee, there is never any guarantee for anything in everyday life. There is no guarantee concerning yourself. The warranties apply only to all the others, those we do not know, those we have not even heard of. There are many people we have never heard of, we may have seen them, but we have rarely heard of them. The rain can be both a plague and a blessing, it's just about the difference between what has been and what's really going to happen. It's not remarkable at all.

The rain is what it is and it's hard to do something about it. Rain does not have any reason to get angry with you. It's always there, whether you want it or not, it is really nothing to do anything about. It has been like this entire last month and that is what you might write a letter home about. But those who live here are already home, those who live here, they have nothing to write home about, they have to stand the sticky heat. They welcome the rain. They hope the rain will clean up the moisture a little. Perhaps it also makes the air a little cooler.

They carry hope, maybe a weak one at that, but hope is that there will be some change. But, like all hope, it is very vague and directed forward in a very fuzzy way. It's like it's not found. The cool weather itself is nothing to long for. The only positive thing about it is that it's not so extremely hot. There are many variables in common. One of them is the guard.

The guard in Paley's Drugstore looks like he is possibly aggressive. He is a black man at around 5 feet 8". Estimatedly, he weighs about 160 pounds. He often moves about in the room, sometimes he is outside the shop. Now he stands still. Most alive in him are his eyes. His eyes are darker than charcoal as they stare at the customers who walk around without hassle on the premises. They take their time waiting for the warm rain to stop. The guard watches two wet, completely soaked, people come in.

One is a man at the age of 30, about six feet and weighing around 200 pounds, some of which do not appear to be compact muscles. But it is always difficult to tell. The guard has made his mistakes in that area before, and discovered his mistake the hard way. Everything is not that simple, that's all. It always seems so simple at first, but once you've studied it a bit closer, you realise that it is more complicated than you first thought. It goes by; and that is the worst.

It's getting more and more confusing. There is not much you can do about it. No more than take on every single day and hope it will not get worse tomorrow. It's the fear that everyday life will become way too complicated that it makes us beg for changes and anything that can interfere with our invasive patterns.

We have far too many such patterns to take into account. The risk is always great that it gets a whole lot worse the day after. It seems that all wickedness can be gathered in piles and falling down on you in a hot melting pot any day. The best part is that you do not know about it in advance. It's always an advantage, so you do not get used to what's coming.

Certainly, the guard is aware of that things may happen at any given moment. That's why he is standing alert and watching the action. But whatever happens he hopes takes place elsewhere and not on his own premises. There it may hopefully be calm and nice. It is always the same view; someone enters who seems to be a righteous citizen, who then pulls out a sawed-off shotgun and it means: farewell to another guard. The guard has looked very attentive, just some moments ago. It is his job to think of traits so that it is possible to describe those who enter the store.

The police will ask him what the customers looked like. The police may be interested in anyone who has been in the shop during the day. The guard cannot remember exactly who. This may happen to every customer entering. He does not know in advance who of those who are a criminal. He does not think he needs to retrieve anything from that man who just came in. He looks like a normal person. But, the risk is there all the time.The other person is a woman just under five feet two, who does not seem to have been starving lately either. Their hair smears against their scalps and they look around.

They walk back and forth in the aisles between the shelves as if they were looking for something special. They pick up the goods and read the packages and they talk to each other. From time to time they wipe the rain from their faces. Their clothes, if possible, are even more wet than their stripy hair. It is as if they've became much more soaked than others customers entering Paley's tonight, like they just have a special ability to attract every aspect of the rain, as if they were particularly vulnerable to the wet weather. Maybe they just had bad luck.

The guard would like them to have had bad luck, he would not like to think people are so undisciplined that they forget to bring rainwear or umbrella when the weather is like it has been lately. He thinks it indicates a bad reality anchorage. He does feel sorry for those who do not really understand what matters.

The guard at Paley's Drugstore wonders why they do not have any rainwear, but he does not care much about it. He has something else to think about. It's only 15 minutes to go until the drugstore closes and maybe another half an hour until they've counted the checkout. Then he steps into the office, fetches the money and carries it to the bank deposit.

Then the day's work is over, then he can relax, maybe watch some football on TV, or have a beer.

Or why not combine both?

People need food, they need medicines, they need a

Vandelier's Song

whole lot of the things that Paley's drugstore provides. They come here when they need those things, they come here for a whole lot of other reasons too, but the important thing is that they come because they need things.

They have a need and Paley's satisfies it. The guard thinks it's like poetry.

"Excuse me, do you have a rest room here?" the woman asks and looks at Vance.

"Sorry, ma'm, you have to go the the restaurant around the corner."

He wonders what's wrong with her, every adult knows that there is no rest rooms in here.

Perhaps she is a foreigner or something? He does not ask, because he simply doesn't care. Of course, there are a lot of commotion in Paley's, it's natural and maybe even inevitable. But he hopes every night that there will not be a real madman. It's going to be nice to come home and rest his swollen feet. Even though he has been on this job for three years now, yes soon four, his feet have not adjusted to standing all day long. They protest almost every night over the treatment he exposes them to.

It has been a quiet day. But he still does not think that the salary from the company compensates for the swollen feet he is going to go home and really soak up in a foot bath. In addition, he has a stiff back, as he also blames on the misery of the job. Perhaps he does not work out enough. He has some bad conscience about that. Good form is also a kind of life insurance. He shrugs. It will turn out well when it's time. All jobs have their drawbacks, this with the feet and the back is something he has to live with.

He knows that he cannot keep up with this job all his life. But right now he sees nothing else that seems attractive enough. The unpleasant thing is that he is really happy with the rest of the life he leads.

He does not have much to complain about. But, despite that, he complains almost every day. Not loud, but he has his thoughts about one problem or another, as we all usually have.

He watches Paterson, the drugstore proprietor, coming in. The Chinese cleaner has already begun his work. He is sweeping the door and smiles and bows to another late customer. The customer looks surprised, looks at the cleaner and then goes on into the store.

One thing is sure, Vance thinks, they are polite anyway, those orientals! He does not know much about them, those he met have never been unpleasant to him. He himself has tried to behave towards them, like against all others.

He must not treat any people different, at least not at work. But he has not found any reason to do it privately either. There has simply never been any reason.

The Chinese cleaner is a recent addition to the staff, the guard no longer remembers what the former cleaner looked like. It's like he no longer exists when he no longer works here. Then there have been many of those who have come and gone, it's as if they disappear out of his memory once they have left Paterson's drugstore.

Jim Vance, 27, the drugstore guard, looks at the late customer. He knows that it's just some who come late to watch and browse stuff. They come in when they think that the cash register is at the fullest. Vance gets worried.

He does not want anything unpleasant to relaxed. He can't afford that. It may be fatal to him.

He has had a quiet and nice day. Just jammed a drunkard, loitering around the shelves and grabbing a couple of cans of soda and some other stuff. The old man was feeble and Vance knows that he lives around the corner so he just told him to go home and take it a little easy.

The old man muttered something, but he smiled at Vance and wanted to shake hands with him. Vance let him do it.

The old man reminded him of his old dad. His dad had died a few years earlier in delirium tremens. Jim Vance does not like any drunkards, but gets upset every time he sees someone who rages a bit or just stands screaming at a street corner.

When the drunks comes in, he gets annoyed by them. Just as they show up, he feels the irritation soaring inside. He tries to check himself, but it's not that easy all the time. For the most part, he succeeds in any case.

He has never been in direct conflict with them, he is well in control of himself.

Sometimes it can be really difficult, it's not always easy to keep his calm. But over the years he has learned a certain measure of mastery. Sometimes he will get a hunch to say or do something, but for the most part he can keep his calm.

There are all kinds of customers coming in, that's why it can be varied to stand here all day long. There is nothing completely similar occurring all of the time, there's something new every day. Jim Vance is grateful for that. If it were not the case, it would be boring to work here. Then he would become more eager to look for something else. Now the months go by, but he's going to make an effort.

Maybe it still indicates that he likes this job? He does not know, has not had much time thinking about it, this is the only job he had for some time.

He worked at the auto factory assembling brake drums, but thought it was boring in the long run. As if this would be so much fun now! It has to be because he has been doing it for so long without having a thought to quit. He just goes on, and it has to mean something.

Jim Vance is watching the newcomer. He stops at a plate of canned potato chips. He keeps on thumbing that can, so that Vance is almost on the verge to go up to him and tell him that this is not a shelter from the warmth.

It usually hurts them! There are not many who want to keep on browsing when Vance's got his eyes on them. But Jim does not have to do anything. Everything solves itself.

The assistant says to the newcomer:

"You get two cans for 95 cents! They're on sale!"

The assistant looks expectantly on the customer. Despite his flaws, Paterson may be a fool of clear-cut on some occasions. Vance thinks it's strange, in itself, but it's not his job to comment on it. He stays in his place and tries to be content with what he has, he does not want to make it more difficult for himself. Jim Vance sometimes becomes weird at heart when he watches the assistant selling stuff to people. Things like Jim thinks it appears they do not need, but they are more or less forced to buy because the assistant is so insistent.

"Okay, I think I'll take two of these."

The newcomer points towards the cans of potato chips. He does not look really happy about getting an opportunity to buy the chips.

Vance is studying the newcomers clothes. The man wears a brownish suit, perhaps to look younger. He seems to be around 40 years old.

It's not easy to determine how old people are. But there are some signs that are always safe. The neck, hands and knees. They reveal more than anything else all together. They give Vance the information he needs.

Vance watches how the soaked couple goes to checkout and pay. They disappear into the rain with a big brown bag that the man wears under his right arm while the woman puts her change into a big black wallet. She seems to have problems with the size of the banknotes and has trouble getting them in the right compartment.

Vance notices that they bought a large bottle of tonic

and a half-gallon pack of vanilla ice cream. He wonders what they're going to do with all that ice cream. Maybe they're going to do some kind of shake, but he does not care any about it all. They are allowed to buy what they want, he has no desire to mess in their food choices. If he did, he would not be alert enough and that could be risky. If he is to be sincere, he usually knows what people entering the drugstore will buy. It's a harmless pastime that has given him many soothing moments. But he must be careful, so he does not loose his attention by keeping too much with that kind of games. It's not like his game to deal with such things, he will ensure that the cash register remains when he leaves when they close or he is released. It's no more noteworthy than that.

When he was younger, much younger, he found it very difficult to know what his peers thought about him. It was not only unpleasant, it even had its clear advantages as well. He did not have to worry much about what they thought. He reckoned he was like he was and did not have to imagine as much as some others. It was good then, but he wondered where it really brought him. What kind of life is he living? Vance has wondered a few times why people buy stuff at the drugstore. It is much more expensive here, because it is kept open so many hours every day. But, there are people who never manage to fit the usual stores' opening hours. Such stores can't do business with people who show up when they're closed.

The man in the brown suit takes the two chip cans

and a bottle of Diet-Pepsi. Vance sees him go to checkout. The man picks up the change and leaves. Paterson, the proprietor, comes up to Vance.

"Okay, Jim, now we close!" Paterson says.

The same thing Paterson says every day makes Vance wonder. Happy that he always carries almost the same expression, and not just the same expression, it is always the same phrase, word for word, every day. It is as though he will never learn anything else, as if he wasn't capable of any other way to express himself in that certain situation.

The Chinese cleaner laughs and says:

"You go, I close from inside!"

Jim likes that the Chinese says something. The first nights he never said a word. It took him a little while. Vance wonders where he's from. Perhaps it has been the same guy all the time. He just hasn't much contact with the cleaners, so there may be reason to suspect that it is the same dude.

"Goodnight, both of you guys!" Paterson says.

He slowly walks away, he has some gait walking through all the premises to make it look like he owns them.

Now, he owns this venue, but Vance has seen him elsewhere, and then he glides in that shabby way too. It's simply Paterson's style. And one thing is certain, you do not complain about his gait to the boss, not unpunished in any case.

"See you tomorrow," Jim mumbles.

He walks towards his car and is really pleased with

his uneventful day. Apart from his swollen feet. But they teach him to live with some discomfort, they are not that painful. He is glad that they work standing on all them days, they are his livelihood, in a manner of speaking.

Therefore, they are important at the same time as they are unimportant. He shrugs and sits down in the car. It's always the same pleasure to sit in a car, it's as if life itself became bigger when you land behind the steering wheel for a ride. He wonders if it is like that or if there is something you pretend to dare to venture out on the streets.

He likes the old car, a Chevrolet, which really has seen better days, but still works well. In any case, he would be hard off to afford another ride. So he is satisfied as long as it rolls without causing too much trouble for him.

When the engine starts, he hears the cracked sound from the tired silencer. He sighs. He will soon have to do something about that silencer.

Sunday Morning

Maybe there was something wrong with the gearbox. The engine nevertheless died and the bus jumped and stopped. Jeff stared at the dashboard and swore. He hit both hands into the steering wheel and swore again. He felt better, but it did not get the car to start right now. He made an attempt to turn the ignition key and the start engine rattled. The engine knocked on and Jeff drove slowly forward.

His converted VW bus slid quietly down the Black Mountain Road. He had left the house on Sundance Drive in a mess. Laverne and the kids were ripping down the walls.

It was not the first time the discharge came in that way. He was a bit depressed over that almost every Sunday started the same. It was as though they could not afford the life they lived.

Sundays have the disadvantage that they're days when you should not be at work. It's just fools who have to go to work during the weekend to get their job done, Jeff thought. But he was hesitant when it came to that. He really did not like to be away from work for too long. Especially not when his Sunday mornings had the peculiarity that they freaked out into some kind of a chaos. This Sunday was a good example of that. Suddenly everything went wrong and he ended up in the car.

Sure, it could have been different, but it was as if a curse hovered over them Sunday mornings. As if they were just miserable and not happy until it was time to go to work on Monday.

It just happened again and again; he fled in his car. Afterwards he did not think there was much he could have done to prevent it from happening. But, sure, he knew. He knew all about that, but it didn't matter; it was still that way it always had appeared to be. But, it seemed like he and Laverne had gotten into a rut that they could not change. A behavior they received with the purchase when they bought the house. A behavior that all their friends also joined. The behavior's none of them wanted, but they were still stuck with.

In a way, he was pleased that it had not gone even worse. He had been mowing the lawn before he fled the field. That would have meant a proper defeat any other day. He was not sure if he should have done it.

He was very doubtful at least. For years he had been very proud that he never hit a woman. But he knew that whatever the law says about such matters it was just a behavior, an alternative way among many others. It was not noble, just one approach.He had chosen not to, but could as well have chosen something else.

There are some days that repeat themselves in a way that makes it impossible to distinguish them from each other; their Sundays were that way. It was simply impossible to separate the past Sundays from each other, they looked so alike to create a certain confusion. Jeff thought they broke into any kind of failure, something that was best to forget as soon as possible. Something it was really no reason to remember.

He sometimes wondered if there were personal defects with him or Laverne, if the kids were wrong, or their way of life. Maybe they had too little money? But they were well off. Certainly there were people who had more money to live on, but many more had it a whole lot worse. Then it could not be that. He could not handle it.

As usual, he had ran his way. Just threw the golf bag in the bus and drove his way. He had been furious until the engine died at the crossroads.

Twin Falls Drive used to be heavily used on weekdays, but he became stressed because it was now too. Anger made him flee.

It used to do just that. He was disappointed that he could not make it disappear while he was angry, but that might be an impossibility.

It may not be possible to quench the anger and irritation while it was in progress.

It is possible that only afterwards, when it died out, you are able to understand what has happened. You may not be able to see yourself objectively even afterwards when it comes to upset emotions.

It's the same every Sunday, he thought, why can not we keep it calm and fine like all other people? Why can't we decide in advance? We know that there comes a Sunday every week.

The kids wanted to go to Sea World and the Laverne to Santa Anna.

"Yes, it doesn't matter. Just let go of all that tinkering," he sighed and turned his head in anger to see if someone followed him on the road and wanted to drive past him.

Having a small bus was no problem in itself, most other cars were equal in size or even bigger. But he was afraid of those people who drive around without any car insurance. You don't want to end up in an incident with such a driver . It can be expensive if you're unfortunate enough.

He drove down to Morell and the little European bus engine spun like a satisfied cat. He was really happy with the bus, used to serve it once a month, and that was much less than the cars he had earlier. It gave him no more worries, no more than you can count on by just owning a car.

There is a set of worries that you never can escape. They gather suddenly at the moment you hand the former owner money for the car. Then the entire package of responsibility and broken parts will throw themselves at you. You are aware of it, but you're just as surprised every time, as annoyed and even angry.

It's unfair, it doesn't matter that everyone else is also affected. They have their problems and you have your own, all alone.

Actually, I would do some work the bus, but it is clear that I would rather take the kids to the fish farm if that's what they want, he thought.

He liked being with them. Especially now, when they gotten so big you could talk to them. When they were smaller, it was not quite fun, although there were moments to remember from that time too. But, it was real fun now.

He had left. Bringing the golf clubs as a kind of excuse. Laverne knew he would be back in a couple of hours and pretend it was exactly what they agreed. Did not seem like she cared. She waited for him like a sniper.

He sometimes grew ill at ease when he thought that Laverne was one of the few people who understood him. But, of course, exercise is proficient and they had been together for awful many years now.

It had started hesitating in a bar quite a few years ago. Their relationship, like some, had grown on them, they had not fought it, and on a beautiful day they sat in a house they owned, together with an understanding bank.

The last few Sunday mornings would be repeated again. They had landed in some kind of strange routine, which made him run away to have some time for himself. It was obvious that he was forced to feel some kind of debt. To make him feel sick trying to feel good.

Of course, neither were the mistakes of Laverne or the kids. Jeff thought they grew apart because they spent too little time with each other. It meant that they did not have such a great desire to spend time together. Laverne thought that kind of reasoning was some kind of amateur psychology, but he did not care. He thought it was enough.

Jeff could as well go down to the golf course. Have a drink and maybe knock off some holes together with the instructor if he was free. Jeff played too rarely to improve his golf; the truth surfaced, he managed to stay at the same level without getting worse.

He constantly realised that he only needed some tips from the instructor to improve his bad playing. But for the most part he was far too busy working. Laverne was on him to start jogging. There was nothing he was looking forward to. The last time he ran was at the university. That was not an experience he would revive.

"Jeff, you're over forty and are starting to put on weight. I don't want you to have a heart attack and die away from me and the kids," Laverne had said.

Jeff felt she'd cornered him there, because he would not either.

But he had tried jogging. It was the most horrific of all the plagues he had come into. In addition, he thought it was boring. Maybe he was born lazy. It's good for all people, he thought, to be born lazy. But, of course, some cover it up really well. They are chasing around all the time. Motivations, work and study to get better in everything. All at the same time. Jeff hoped that such types of heart-attacks are affected and that doctors force them to deal with too many things at the same time. But he has very little hope of getting the support from the doctor's office. It was far too health-free. But, it's their job to talk about things time after time, it's nothing Jeff can do anything about.

He did not even have the energy to think about it seriously.He turned into Little Meadow Farm. It was quite some time since someone used the field for farming. Bannisters had built the golf course long before leasing it to the club. It had obviously been done on a chance, but since there was no other course in the immediate vicinity, it was obvious that the interest was great. At least there were a lot of people playing during the weekends.

It was a nice little course.

Jeff had been playing there for a couple of years and gotten to know some of the members. It was like a neighborhood club. There were no real aces on golf, except the instructor. And that made you feel good to play there for the most part. When Jeff took the golf bag out of the bus and walked up to the clubhouse, he saw Chance Delaney arriving in his car. Delaney always kept the latest model. Jeff wondered if it really was working out as well for him as it appeared. But, Delaney chose what he put his money on.

"Hi, Jeff!" Chance hollered.

Chance was one of those people who thought it was weird of Jeff to have a bus. So he always had a comment about that bus. He used sometimes to call Jeff for Beetle-Jeff.

Named after a car! Jeff used to think in his darkest moments. But he did not take it that seriously. What does a name, a nickname, mean? He tried to regard it as an expression of friendship from Delaney's side. In all other ways it would be difficult to deal with.

"On the run from the wifey and the kids?" Chance wondered when he got out of the car.

He looked rudely fresh and really trimmed. Jeff felt

a sting of jealousy, but if he did not look as fresh as Chance, he only had himself to blame, he thought.

"Yes, actually," Jeff answered and put his golf bag on the white gravel.

It crashed a bit against the gravel. He did not care that the bag became dusty. He could wipe that off later.

"Shall we leave now?" Chance suggested and put his golf bag so that it rested on the top of his shoes. Jeff noticed that Chance was taking care of his stuff. He might have to take on that part of Chance's behavior.

"Alright! Had really thought of getting hold of the instructor. But you play better than me, so I can learn from you instead," Jeff said generously.

Jeff pulled out a club and saw that he forgot to fix the broken winding on the shaft. He must remember to fix it to the next round.

"Sure, I'm your man!" Chance noted in his usual manner.

His clubs were certainly in perfect condition, like Chance himself. Jeff felt like something very old and very moldy. He wondered what had come over him, did he break down?

"As hard headed as always!" Jeff muttered, "what do you know, maybe I've become a class better lately?"

He swung the shameful club easily back and forth. It seemed like it would be possible to play with the broken winding this time too.

"It's not enough to become one class better," Chance said, smiling, but not without a streak seriousness.

"You need to be best in class to take me!"

"God, you're so evil!" Jeff noted.

He sometimes felt badly opposed to others' frenzy. It was not something he would like to emphasise himself. Although, of course, there were those who thought even Jeff was a freaky bastard.

"I was only just joking," Chance said.

He lifted the golf bag and put it by the strap over his shoulder. Jeff saw that he did not lean his body sideways. It seemed like that bag did not weigh anything. Could he really be in such a good shape?

"Okay," Jeff smiled.

But on the inside he felt quite worried. He wondered why Chance seemed to be in such good shape.

It seemed unfair, maybe he would start jogging, and make Laverne impressed looking at his body again.

They carried their bags to the tee of first hole's after paying.

There were not many people on the course yet. It was cool and nice weather. As made for golf, or a family outing.

"How many shall we play?" Chance wondered.

Chance put his bag down and Jeff noticed that he looked completely unwinded, while he himself felt a little out of breath. This seemed to be a hard marble to crack!

"I only have time with three to four holes," Jeff said, "then I have to go home and make peace with my family again."

Jeff must at least strive a bit, could not just let everything fall apart. It seemed too childish.

"It's only half past nine," Chance said, "can we say six holes and the winner is invited to a drink?"

He tilted his head and looked at Jeff, in a way that Jeff felt dizzying to come from a man.

"Okay," Jeff said.

He imagined that it was him who would be the one who had to pay for those drinks. However, there is nothing free in life. Those who believe it have not seen life as it is.

They played out.

Chance placed his ball 20 yards from the green. Jeff ended up in the sand pit 80 yards behind Chance. It was no start Jeff was pleased with. Not at all. On the third hole Jeff had a fabulous luck. He played out on the third hole, and the ball bounced against a tree trunk and suddenly entered the track again. The fact that Chance got away properly also helped. Then it did not seem as if he really got away from the adversity. After six played holes they were even and it was Jeff's first time keeping up with Chance.

"Should we also take seventh, or will we share the winner's fee?" Chance wondered.

Jeff liked to track some bitterness in his voice, but it could as well be his own joy over his success that made his ears a bit hypersensitive.

"I'm quite happy," Jeff replied with badly hidden delight.

He had always been bad at playing poker and other games that required you to keep a blank face. He was simply too primitive for such exercises.

"Clearly you're happy when you played on par with me," Chance laughed.

Jeff listened carefully if there was any bitterness in Chance's voice, but could not trace anything indicating that. Perhaps it was all just pure imagination from his side. He himself would have been irritated over a similar development, but Chance might be made of harder stuff.

"Yes, I'll have a drink to celebrate. So you can feel like the real winner."

Jeff really thought he could hold that deal, because he felt confident he could put out Chance again. He felt he was aggressive and chiseled. Chance would not be a match for him today.

"Okay, for now," Chance said dryly.

Chance seemed mad about something, but Jeff had no desire or power to trod into it, right now he had a handful of his own problems.They walked up to the parking lot and put the bags in the cars before going to the clubhouse. They stayed for a short while. They each ordered beer and poured them down quickly. On the way out to the cars, Chance asked:

"Did you argue with the wife?"

He looked at Jeff, as if to spy any annoying disaster, as if he really cared about what Jeff was doing. Of course it was pure nonsense, he did not give a damn about what Jeff and his family were doing. Perhaps it was only a way to be polite or something. Jeff did not know.

"Yes, but it's nothing serious."

Now, at least, he was convinced that it was not. He knew it would be fine; just as it had always worked out when there was a bull on the line between them there at home. It had become so predictable that it was sad to live with it. But you persevere, you persevere.

"Fine, I'll see you next Sunday," Chance said, and patted Jeff lightly on the shoulder in the old customary manner.

Chance had a habit of caressing people in that male, somewhat crazy way. Jeff did not really like it, but handled it, it was a ritual. There were much worse things he had to deal with.

"Sure, you'll get a beating," Jeff laughed.

He did not really reflect on what he said, it just slipped out of him out of old habit. It was probably the old usual jaw tradition that he wanted to maintain in some way. At least he did not think it would give Chance's next reply.

Jeff had never been very quick to really reply and probably did not understand how other people could take the opportunity in flight and get a bang on what they said, even though Chance might not be a heavy hitter at all.

"Oops, you won't win. It was I who celebrated the victory, right?" Chance laughed.

He was tapping a golf club into the grass, an bad habit that Jeff had a lot of trouble to deal with. That was not the way he would handle a club himself. Never ever, but he did not want to argue with how Chance handled his clubs, it had been obvious, he thought and felt noble.

"I was just kidding," Jeff said.

But he did not feel that certain when he drove away from the golf course. It was as if it still meant a lot for him to go even with Chance. Badly enough. He had never been much to compete in that funny way that many of his friends were up to. He did not want to throw himself into challenges that were just for fun.

It seemed so futile and cool that he never managed to mobilise any interest in it. However, there were so many others who made it happen that there were races all the time in all areas of life. When the VW-bus swung into Sundance Drive, Jeff was calm. He parked in the street, carried the golf bag into the garage and entered the house. It was worryingly quiet. It was so quiet that he first thought that the whole gang had gone away, but he heard sound from the living room.

"Santa Anna or Sea World?" he asked Laverne when he entered the living room.

He gave her a hug that she did not try to avoid. Jeff thought it was a victory, already. But he did not pull too much weight on it. He knew it did not matter, Laverne was not calculating in that way.

"Sorry I got angry before," he said.

It did not feel like great fun to return home after the magnificent run he did a few hours ago. It was a bit of a anti-climax to pop up here at home again. He had never gotten used to the fact that you can not really escape from everyday life. It is there all the time and bind you to other people, to routines, to things you promised to do when you are in another mood and forced to do when you are in yet another mood. In short, it's hell and it's strange that people stand to live that way year after year.

"It doesn't matter. Now the kids want to go to Santa Anna," she laughed.

Jeff could not detect any clue in her voice, but he could be wrong.She was not easy to understand, that Laverne. Perhaps it was the trait in her character that once made her so irresistible to him. Maybe there was something else, but he could very well imagine that it was that hard-mindedness that had tricked him, among other things.

There are some days that repeat in a way that makes it impossible to distinguish them from one another; their Sundays were like that. It was simply impossible to separate the past Sundays from one another, they looked confusingly identical.

Now, Jeff thought that there was some hope for their Sundays, at least in the end this Sunday. He hoped it would do the next Sunday as well. He could only hope.

"Shall we leave now or right away?" Jeff laughed and gave her a hug.

Laverne hugged him back, in the old invasive manner he learned to enjoy for so many years. He almost got a lump in his throat.

"They probably are already in the car," Laverne said, leaving him to go to the kitchen, "I'll just pick up the picnic!"

"Did you bribe them to change their minds?" Jeff laughed.

He did not feel completely sure how or what she had done, but it did not seem to be a major problem. At least Laverne smiled. And that was a good sign.

An Unusual Day, Judy!

Judy Gardner felt quite empty inside. It was as though she had been hollowed out from within. She did not understand what was happening. As tired as she was, she did not really care anymore about that either. She just wanted to go to bed. There was forgetfulness in bed.

Coffee shops really are places for people who cannot find anything to do with the time they do not have to work. It is strange that some other people go to such places, though. Take for example this woman who comes in through the door! Why is she sitting here on a day like today? Doesn't she have any more important things to do?

Who wants to find out is not as interesting as the question, or maybe, the answer. It is interesting to know why some people do things that others might not even imagine.

Perhaps she is here just because she really does not have better things to do with herself. It is not always certain that all people always behave as rationally and thoughtfully as you would imagine.

Most often, people live their lives in a much rougher way than they would like. Suddenly life is over and you may have wasted it. For those who hang around in cafes it is the same. In some way, the cafes can be quite different, now it's not, but it can come happen any century. The cafe hides its visitors away from the everyday life going on just outside it's doors. It is the main task of the café, as well as serving coffee and bread of all kinds. The café lives its own life among all the other attractions that compete for people's attention.

It is the light that makes the whole difference, nothing else. The light in the cafés makes you look alive in a different way than you usually do in the open air, with the daylight whipping into your eyes. Perhaps it's the light that does it, but it's not certain; there are cafes where you sit down outside. But, sure enough there is something in it?

Light is of outmost importance when you feel low. Some claim that there is the lack of light that makes you depressed. Others mean that you avoid the light since the depression makes you want to hide. It does not matter anyway. The important thing is that the light is of great importance when you are depressed.

Just like the light brightens when you want to see things, it reveals things that you do not want others to see. It even reveals things that you want to hide for yourself, and it makes the light both a friend and an enemy, like so much else. It makes you look upon light in at least two ways, it can be tamed, but it may attack at any time and you never know when it happens. That is cruel.

In the cafeteria, it was sparsely populated when Judy Gardner settled down at a plastic table designed for four with her coffee and her donut. In the yellow light from the well-lit fluorescent lamps in the ceiling she looked worn out. It was nothing out of the ordinary. At least not during the last six months it had not been. Probably she would have looked tired in any lighting.

Only, those fluorescent tubes made her look more tired than she ought to. Now you may not really decide how tired someone will look like, but you can say that someone looks more tired than what seems healthy. This woman did. She should not sit here, she should be at home and fast asleep, but she was really tired. Bill had told her in the morning that she ought to get to bed earlier in the evenings.

It is the most common advice for those who look down and out in one way or another. It's not easy to decide what makes people slouch like withering flowers. So, the easiest way is to ask them to sleep more. Then, at least, you have given them some kind of good advice. Then it's on their own accord to follow it or reject it. It's not like the adviser's thing to decide, but, it's easy to argue like that when you're sitting in front of the table with the beer can in your fist and watching the midnight movie.

Judy was not so interested in watching television, she seldom watched. Certainly it happened, but then it would be an exciting movie like 'Sierra Madre's Treasure' with Humphrey Bogart or the like. Otherwise, it didn't matter, she thought.

Judy was even busy trying to spice up their apartment. She read about different ways to make the living room more stylish. She learned a lot of tricks to make great changes with little money, like how to build a spice cabinet yourself from old fruit cases.

Judy started a lot of these do it yourself schemes. Some of them became nothing, but others she managed to implement. She could experience a feeling of being unsuccessful at times, especially when she did something that would not work or looked like nothing an adult person had built. To be honest, Judy managed to finish a lot of what she did start. She had a lot of things she wanted to finish, many projects going on, but it happened so much that took the stamina out of her that she was having trouble implementing what she wanted to accomplish.

Judy succeeded for the most part, that was not it, but she thought everything should move on much faster and more easily, but she thought she mostly was struggling in headwinds, and that the apartment started to be a bit like she wanted it. Of course, there was always as much that remained. She was still unhappy with how the bathroom looked like. In the bathroom she had forced herself to set up new tiles. It had taken her a whole weekend.

At first, she thought she was good at it, but she soon changed her mind. She had asked Bill to come and have a look. He would just peek at the movie until the next commercial.

That was his usual comment. He would always just peek at the movie or football match he watched. He was not interested enough in her to even interrupt his comfort for a while. He was sticking to that TV-bitch, as though it forced him to watch, Judy did not understand it.

She was disappointed in his lack of interest. But after a five minutes he appeared. She had almost given up hope.

Bill threw a quick glance at her tiles and said:

"It's a bit uneven above the sink!"

And then he disappeared towards his television set again. She could easily have killed him then. After a few weeks, she also realised that it was a little askew just above the washbasin. But not only there. it was lacking lines and was askew everywhere.

She sensed her inability to cope with life in everything she did. She thought it was strange that she did not manage to do anything properly. But it was as though all her newly started projects demanded to be done very quickly and then you had to accept that it became a bit slanted and tilted, she thought. Or, she'd thought like that until recently. Then she had come across other thoughts.

In the cafeteria, under the yellow light, in the air filled with fumes from roasting burgers, only a faint thought of the failed bathroom remains. Now it does not bother her that much. Now she has new plans for the bathroom. Now it is not only a failure, but also an opportunity to achieve something. She feels intoxicated by her new insight.

Judy is not happy about it, but the bathroom is not here in the cafeteria at Sears department store. She just happens to sense it flickering in her mind. She does not know when she will have time and energy to do something about that tile work. It's not just that she's sad because she failed. You have to be entitled to fail at what you do, otherwise you should never venture into something new. You would just love to walk around in the same ordinary steps as always. But she is not satisfied. Now it's just some coffee break. In a few minutes she will pull in a pair of carts of goods that have been out of stock. Then it is time to go home. Home to the failed bathroom. Home to Bill, who will be sitting in front of the television set as usual, with a beer in his hand.

She does not know why he is not interested in anything but the television set and that one-of-a-kind beer. She might ask him one day, ask him where to the old, fancy Bill disappeared. Where did the old fancy Judy disappear? She does not know that either. She lights a cigarette, takes some gulps of coffee. It's already almost cold. Everything is against her today, even the coffee cools faster than usual.

She sees that Mr. Kowalski is glancing at her from the door of the store room across the street. She puts out the cigarette into the coffee after having a last gulp.

The filter on the cigarette sucks up the coffee. It happens very fast and the paper around the filter falls off on one side.

She picks up the cigarette pack as she walks towards the store room door. She is silent, she has plenty of time.

It's not that much fun in the storeroom that she volunteers rapidly in there.

"Long breaks," Mr. Kowalski mumbles when Judy enters the storeroom.

Judy stares at him, but Kowalski has already turned away. Perhaps he didn't even look at Judy when he made that comment.

Judy puts the cigarette pack back into her jeans pocket and walks to one of the trolleys with cartons. The labels on the cartons state that they contain sheets. That at least explains why the cartons are so dramatically heavy. It seems like there would be lead in those cartons when she has to lift them. Judy is wondering who will sleep on these sheets in the future? Judy thinks; not me anyway. There are too many sheets. I would never have time to use so many even if I changed bed linen every day during the rest of my life! Well, maybe not, but …

She wonders what kind of patterns are on the sheets, or if they are solid colored. It is not apparent from the images on the cartons what the sheets look like.

"Here we go!" Kowalski shouts with his usual annoying and angry voice.

Judy is wondering if his wife does not let him sleep with her. He sounds frustrated, to say the least. But maybe it's not her job to lay down how they have it in bed at home.

In addition, she does not see that much action in her own bed, so it's really like a pot calling the kettle black.

"Okay, okay," Judy snaps and hurries forwards, she feels worn out in some way.

It is not the usual common fatigue you experience when working hard. This is something else. Years of disappointments begin to take their toll on her now. Only now have all the adversities grown enough to completely destroy her. She sighs at the thought of the past, does not even want to think about the future.

She pushes the trolley into the store room. The color of the cartons shows which shelves she shall put them on. Judy does not like that part of the job right now. The fork truck she usually uses is broken; has been broken for four days now. It does not seem like it should be repaired this week.

Now, Judy has to lift the cartons herself and it's hard work, she thinks. There are 48 cartons on each trolley and she has to lift them up on shelves that are three feet high. It takes its toll on her back and arms.

Judy is angry. Suddenly, it dawns on her how much she has been through the years. It makes her really angry. She does not realise that she could just stay being silent and take all that crap from all possible and impossible people.

She is very pissed off.

When the cartons start to slide down from the trolley, she gets really upset. The cartons fall unto the cracked concrete floor with dull thumps.

Then she breaks inside. Then the last thump makes her nerves burst. She lets the inner rage flow and releases her withdrawn anger.

"I can't take this crap anymore!" she yells, "you don't pay me enough!

She slams her hands to her face and starts to cry. It is no violent weeping, but it's at least some salty tears breaking away below her eyelids. Judy feels so ignored and misunderstood that nothing matters anymore. Now she doesn't care about anything at all.

Now she just wants to be weak and weep. There is not much else to choose from.

"So, so, look," she hears Kowalski.

He puts his arm around her shoulders and fondles her head. Judy flinches, like she burnt herself on something. But Kowalski holds a firm, but not very intrusive grip around her shoulders. She does not struggle to get free, but her heart beats faster than ever.

"Let me be," Judy whispers.

He threatens her, just by standing so close to her that he can touch her. She simply is not used to someone getting so close to her at work.

It scares her pretty much. She would rather just fly away from this situation. She wants to go away and does not really care what the consequences may be. It does not matter anymore.

She's past that point now. It might have been much more important just a few days ago. Now it has almost no significance anymore.

"Take it easy," Kowalski says, "just take it easy, I didn't mean to be rough on you when you came in here. It came out worse than I meant."

"I know," Judy mumbles.

She starts to calm down, it is no longer that awkward when he is holding her. She's getting used to it, she thinks. In any event, the heart is no longer jumping out of her body.

"Take care with the cartons. Nobody will thank you for wearing yourself out by lifting them," Mr. Kowalski says.

Now she sensing like a void around them, as if they were the last people in the world. Mr. Kowalski and her, it would not have been her first choice if she had planned for the future.

"Why doesn't Paterson let anyone fix the fork lift then?" she wonders, a little childish, she thinks.

She takes a look at Mr. Kowalski. He suddenly looks nice.

"I agree with you. He should fix that truck. It's wrong for you to work more because he doesn't see to it," Kowalski mutters.

Judy looks at Kowalski. With surprise.

Kowalski has indeed changed! It's like she can't really believe it's the same man she has worked with for six months and who never said a kind word to her

"You are so different today, Mr. Kowalski," Judy sighs.

She is disappointing herself, she sounds like a goose out of any 1930s movie. She doesn't mind 1930s movies, but she doesn't want to sound like a goose from any of them. She can do just fine without it.

"Do you really think so, Mrs. Gardner?" Kowalski laughs.

Judy is wondering if this isn't the first time she's seen Mr. Kowalski laugh properly, as by relief. They may not have had anything to laugh at before. In any case, nothing to laugh at together. She wonders why it was that way. She feels slightly humbled by Mr. Kowalski's transformation. Maybe she can change herself too.

"Yes, you are so kind," she smiles.

Judy does not really understand what happened to her. Above all, she does not understand what happened to the surly and one-sided Kowalski.

"Maybe it's because today is really the first time we actually talk to each other," Kowalski says, smiling at her, yes, this is probably the first time he's smiling at her too, it's a very unusual day.

"Maybe so," says Judy, she is starting to get used to the new Kowalski now, but yet not quite. We all need time to get used to learning what changing conditions mean.

"Of course it is," Kowalski says, "we have been working together for half a year and only just argued with each other. We have never said a honest word to each other."

"What the hell is going on here?" Paterson wonders, sticking his head into the warehouse.

Paterson is crimson red in the face, doesn't seem to be in a particularly good mood, but it's nothing new. He is rarely in a good mood.

Judy senses that she slips away a bit, but Kowalski's grip on her shoulders becomes a little harder.

He doesn't let her back away from Paterson.

"We wonder!" Kowalski says, "why you didn't fix Mrs. Gardner's truck?"

Kowalski glares angrily at Paterson, with an intensity Judy has never seen before.

"Well, I forgot about that," says Paterson, "it should be arranged in the morning, Kowalski!"

It sounds like Paterson is trying to make an effort, but it is easy to talk, it does not commit to much. It may be forgotten tomorrow.

"The poor woman has worn herself out trying to lift those boxes," Kowalski states.

Most of the anger has disappeared from his voice, but he has not really become as gentle as before.

"Mrs Gardner, take the rest of the day off, and the truck will be ready in the morning. I'm really sorry, but I totally forgot about all this," Paterson says, seemingly sincere.

Judy does not realise that there is such a person behind the mask, whom they call Paterson every day, that he is also some ordinary kind of man. It hasn't been clear to her until now.

"That's just how it is supposed be," Kowalski says, winking at Judy.

When Paterson leaves, Kowalski says:

"It really seems like he's not completely impossible anyway, or what do you say?"

Kowalski stares at her, in a friendly way she didn't think he would have been able to. Judy is simply damn surprised at the transformation Kowalski has shown.

"No," Judy laughs, "there's probably some hope for him too. Thank you, I don't understand why I haven't told him before."

She smiles at Kowalski. It feels like they have been friends for a long time. Maybe they have been that too, without daring to admit it, or because they have not told each other that they need to be friends.

"I did only that much," Kowalski laughs, "go home and rest and when you're rested, you will see that there will be speed in Paterson until tomorrow!"

Judy does as he says and gets out of the warehouse. She calmly walks towards home. There is no need to rush. She has no reason to work her ass off for anyone. No one orders her to do it, but something within her more or less forces her forward so that she will end up completely down and out.

When Judy comes home, she is determined to tear down the tiles in the bathroom and put them back up. Plastered right this time. Now it feels like she has both the time and the energy to cope. She won't care about Bill's comments. Not one of them

"How was work?" Bill wonders from in front of the television.

It is as if she has suddenly become a entirely different person. Not that she has changed fundamentally, but she has seen another way of life, another meaning to her existence. She feels almost hopeful. This is the first time in a very long time that she has felt that way.

Judy thinks it's weird that it's really the first time in a long time that she's feeling so well. It's sad if you think about the past, but it is promising for the future.

It could have been much worse. She is happy it is not. So very happy. She somehow feels uplifted by

110

what happened during the day. The reason is that even in her wildest dreams she could never have imagined that it could be different at work. It would be grey and sad and that was just not the case anymore. So she had imagined that her life would be forever grey in the future.

But life has changed, the light has changed, so that almost all of the shadows have disappeared, or at least changed their intensity. Judy is less tired. As if the very feeling of light would make you feel more at ease.

Light is of the outmost importance when you feel depressed. Some claim that it is the lack of light that makes you depressed. Others believe that you flee the light because the depression causes you to want to hide. It does not matter now, in any case.

At first she does not intend to answer Bill, it does not feel important anymore, but then she still thinks she can do it.

She thinks that she can as well offer it to him. Not because he deserves it, but still.

"As usual," Judy says, but she smiles as she walks out of the bathroom.

It's been quite a long time since she smiled that way. It is about whether all of life has changed. During just one single day. She likes it.

She really likes it.

Roses & Perfume

Some days, it is as if life suddenly becomes more tangible, more real. Maybe it has something to do with how old you are when you experience such a day. Maybe age doesn't matter. Maybe you can be any age.

For Lucille Meyer, age didn't matter. She wasn't worried about how old people were. Not even about how old she herself was, she had not had the privilege of being old. Maybe she wouldn't get that benefit either. Being old is more a feeling than a physical stage. There are people who are born old, or at least with an ageing soul.

It has nothing to do with the actual age. Lucille Meyer tried to avoid falling into that trap. It wasn't something she was looking forward to. But for some it was a goal in itself to grow old.

She didn't understand them.

If you think too much about the past, you cannot overlook the present, she thought. It was her way of managing life for herself. She hadn't learned it from anyone, it was something she had come up with. She wasn't proud of it.

She just noted that things were the way things were. More was not the case.

Lucille Meyer was 22. It wouldn't have mattered if she was only 16. Lucille had never been a child. Sure, she had been small and helpless for a while, but she considered it as just a phase she was going through.

Lucille just grew up and got older. Her parents now belonged to the past. When she left home at the age of 18, she erased their faces from her memory. It was a very deliberate act and she had realised that this was what you had to do to avoid drowning by their care.

She had never owned a photo of them. She never thought of contacting them again. She was sure that she would succeed in living up to her intentions, she had not one doubt on that point.

Lucille had always been very determined and stubborn. It was the only thing she brought with her from home. However, she doubted that it was an inheritance from her shillyshally parents. They had not very much to decide on and therefore learned to decide on something.

A year passed and she held on to her intentions, just as she had decided. She had heard that they were looking for her on some occasions, but Lucille had properly covered the tracks behind her.

They couldn't get hold of her. She had been preparing for such a long time that she would have been surprised, very surprised, if they found her. She was glad that she had managed to cut them off so well, she would have been very disappointed if they got in touch with her. Imagine if you would not succeed in something you set out to do, she occasionally thought and got cold chills at the thought.

She did not want to look upon herself as a failure.

She saw herself as a human being at the beginning of a career.

A lot had happened in the rather short time that had passed, it had changed her completely. She thought she had traveled lightyears from the little hole in the ground where she had grown up. Lucille had gotten a job, had been kicked out of it because she didn't want to put up with the foreman's very special ideas about what her duties would be. As resolute as she had left her parents, she left her first job. She didn't even have time to worry about the future. She didn't have to because she lived completely in the present.

The future does not exist, she told herself every morning, the future is what we create by just being ourselves!

Whenever she dwelled about what had been, it was without regrets. It was as if those years on the farm had been just about waiting. As if it was only for her to become so grown up that she was allowed to take care of herself. That she became a citizen in the eyes of society and did not have her parents as a ballast.

It went on for a month. It may have been more than a month, but that's how she thought of the past, when it appeared at some point, as an indefinite period of time. Then she fell by chance upon the used books, among the dust and relative stillness.

Her job was to sell, unpack the incoming books and manage the bookkeeping. Mr. Partridge acquired the books himself. It was probably the only thing he was really interested in. To buy more books and to read them. Mr. Partridge did not want to get separated from a book he thought seemed interesting before he had read it himself.

Then it went very dire with the business.

At first Lucille thought Mr. Partridge was a strange man. It was as if all the books in the world were looking to meet him. He seemed to feel a compulsion to read them all, as if he were consumed by a hunger, or rather, a quest for the ultimate book, the book that would give him answers to all the questions he was asking.

"Don't sell those," Mr. Partridge could say, making a hefty sweeping gesture, which Lucille Meyer interpreted as applying to all books in the store. And it did in a manner. She understood him, but at the same time as she realised the shop would go into the drains if she did like he wanted.

"No, Mr. Partridge," she replied as an obedient employee, but she secretly sold his books, otherwise Mr. Partridge would soon have no customers left.

He probably wouldn't have a place to read them either, if he got like he wished. The business was dependent on at least some money coming in. Only buying books creates no wages.

Apropos salaries, she wondered if Mr. Partridge paid himself any wages. It didn't seem that way. But it could be that she did not have full transparency into the accounting.

Although she was sure she was keeping track of how bad things were for Mr. Partridge. There could be no other accounting than the one she did for him. He was too impractical to cope.

Mr. Partridge was simply a very impractical man, he had his knowledge of books, but life in general did not seem to interest him. He seemed to enjoy the order of things he created around himself. It also suited Lucille quite well.

She did her part and Mr. Partridge was glad he didn't have to do it himself, Lucille fixed the bookkeeping and discouraged the customers who wanted to buy certain books Mr Partridge had let her understand that he did not want to be separated from. They did not talk at all that often, but liked each other in their own way. It was as if they understood each other without having to use many words. Lucille liked Mr. Partridge more than any other adult she had ever met. Not that she found him particularly attractive, she had completely different demands on men as prospective lovers. But there was something about Mr. Partridge that made her stay in the store without experiencing any distinct discomfort at the thought of having to stay there for a year or two.

When Lucille Meyer looked at the clock above the shelf with foreign literature, it was already half past twelve. She cursed Mr. Partridge. It was his unreadable hand-writing she had to thank for sitting here in the middle of the night. But of course she was paid to rewrite his scribbles into something that at least had a remote resemblance to accounting.

She wondered in the stillness of her mind how he had

Vandelier's Song

managed to convey this before she appeared on stage. He had let her realise that she was the first help he had for many years. Perhaps he lied. Or he would have stumbled his way through it for the clean ride. The IRS were not to play with when it came to accounting, but he had apparently succeeded in one way or another. It was very strange.

Lucille understood from the numbers she purportedly wrote that there was no brilliant business to sell and buy used books like Mr. Partridge did. He himself sat mostly behind the counter in the antique store on Dumaine Street and read in some old tome instead of luring customers into the store.

Modern methods such as advertising and the like did not seem to be methods he had even heard about. He seemed to live in a world that was hopelessly outdated. But Lucille Meyer managed on her salary and she enjoyed her work. The only thing that worried her was that she had to get out of the antique store on Dumaine Street and go out into the world before it became too much of a safe spot for her.

Lucille was not a big woman. She was tender. Some of her friends called her Petite. But what she lacked in scope, she compensated with her stubbornness. Her friends were amazed that so much momentum could be hidden in such a small body.

She had decided to get Mr. Partridge's papers in order this evening and was soon able to do so. It was just a matter of another hour's work, then the tax collector would have nothing to comment on.

Now she realized at least that she had to return to the pile of paper the next day. It was not with light heart that she imagined a continuation of this work. She put a book over the paper and wrote a note to Mr. Partridge.

"Don't touch those papers!"

Lucille put out the lamp over the desk. The shop looked very strange when it got dark. All the destinies and thoughts that existed in all those books seemed to come out of their hiding places from between the dusty covers. They stepped out to live their own lives when they were at last alone in the room.

It was as if those old books only really came alive when darkness surrounded them. Lucille shrugged. It was probably only her imagination gifting her with one more of the usual pranks. She was not particularly interested in books. To her, they were a commodities like any other commodity.

She stepped out through the cramped doors of the antique shop. It felt undeniably less hot outside them, though it was probably just imagination, too. The heat at this time of year could be as pervasive as a peddler in the street.

Strange that no one kicks in these doors and takes what is in here, she thought, but of course, the only thing in here are books.

Well, no one here in New Orleans would think of stealing some cheap used books. But who knows, she thought, there are real fanatics when it comes to old books too! She had met some of them in the antique shop. Some of them really scared her. Even though she was stubborn herself, some of those people showed a stubbornness that bordered on madness.

Lucille could not understand why an old book could make the eyes glitter on those book collectors. But sometimes they could barely come to their senses again after they had found something they had been looking for during years. They seem to turn into small kids.

She stepped out into Dumaine. It was as dark as usual, the streetlights doing their best to at least punch small holes in the massive blanket of darkness. But it was still a compactness of dark surrounding her. Darkness is as natural a part of Louisiana nights as jazz is part of Vieux Carré. She never really participated in the night life. Most of it was for the tourists. They came here from all over the world just to walk on Bourbon Street. She thought they had lost their marbles, all of them.

Lucille thought of Mark as she walked up Bourbon Street. He had returned after being away from town for several years. Those who met him said he was wearing some kind of colorful hippie clothes. He had apparently hibernated with some lingering hippie colony somewhere. Someone said he had met his former wife again. Lucille had never known him very well. She had met him at a few parties just when she was new in town. That was before they discontinued the trams and replaced them with buses. It didn't matter to her. But she met people who cried themselves silly over the lost trams as if they had been real life and the buses just a bad replacement. She wondered if it had been just as much rubbish talk when the old horse trams once disappeared.

Bourbon was alerted by the usual selection of sex shows and music, food and some kind of art adapted for the tourists, magicians and drinks. All to turn the eyes of everyone who came to town to experience the cradle of jazz. Lucille did not listen to jazz, she was not that interested in music over all. Sometimes, when she was trying to be honest with herself, she realised that the only thing that interested Lucille Meyer was herself and how her life would develop. Everything else was just some sort of back drop in the Lucille Meyer Story. She assumed it was the same for everyone. They were only interested in themselves, them   too.

She walked almost straight into a woman standing in the middle of Bourbon singing an old song about love and roses while holding a lone red rose in her hand. The singing girl was dressed in black bolero, a thin white blouse, short black skirt and gold colored boots. The woman looked like the spitting image of whores Lucille had met during her time in New Orleans.

"Do you want to buy a rose, ma'am?" the woman asked, stretching a rose towards Lucille, but Lucille was not interested.

What would she do with a rose? In addition, she could certainly buy a similar rose for a fifth of the price the singing woman wanted. Lucille passed the woman without responding. She was fully occupied trying to avoid bumping into people who were on their way to and from bars and restaurants.

All apparently with some glasses internally and hot with the fever from the music that now rolled out on Bourbon.

For years, they have been listening to the music at home on their turntables in big cities and country houses around the world before one day coming to New Orleans to listen to the "real jazz."

It was a strange world to her. She couldn't even remember if she was listening to music when she was growing up. It was a thing that never really interested her. A closed door of sorts.

St. Peter Street was quiet. At least compared to Bourbon. Lucille lived upstairs at the corner of Basin and Canal, so she didn't have much of a distance to walk. Despite the buzz of pocket thieves and ordinary confidence tricksters, she was not afraid to walk home alone at night.

Only once it happened that she became involved in something more exciting than that the men gave her offers that she could ignore by just continuing to walk. Down at Jackson Square, a man had pulled her into a gate. When she started screaming, he immediately released her arm and said:

"Take it easy, I don't want to hurt anyone!"

Then he wandered away through the ocean of people and disappeared out of her sight. It was as if he had never even touched her. She did not even reflect on how she would have reacted if he had switched on aggression of some kind.

It wasn't for her to speculate. She handled reality just

as she met it, she didn't add anything on her own. She realised she had far too little imagination to do that.

Lucille liked the color of the street lights and the neon signs against the bright house walls and the dark sky high above her. The relative coolness of the evenings gave her a sense of freedom. It was as if the coolness was a promise that life could go on forever, as if it could even get better if you just bided your time.

Maybe it was a way to con herself, but she liked it a bit. It appealed to her trust in the future, though she couldn't imagine exactly what that future would look like.

That coolness reminded her of a bygone era, and precisely the difference between then and now made her feel so free that sometimes she couldn't help but smile to herself. Whoever saw her smile with the neon light flashing across her face probably couldn't help but smile back at her. She seemed to enjoy her life. In a way that one should treat all people to enjoy their lives. A man came walking towards her. He stood out from the crowd in that, despite his well-pressed light suit, he was either ill or very badly intoxicated. He leaned against the walls of the house and had clearly difficulties to walk along St. Peter.

Lucille did not look very hard at him, it was not unusual to see people intoxicated in Vieux Carré. But she noticed him, she did. It would have been strange otherwise. He was a stately man and Lucille Meyer was no younger than that her eyes when there was something to look at started noticing. She lived the life of a spinster. Sure, there were occasional men, but that wasn't enough of that item to make her really happy. But she was careful not to become too obsessed with anyone. It would only slow her down.

So, Lucille looked around and liked some of what she saw. It wasn't that he was drunk, since drunk is of a transient nature and if the rest was okay, then drunk could be taken with the purchase. She smiled to herself, but when the man passed her and suddenly turned and went back the same way he had come, she lost interest in him.

She felt a little tired and thought it would be nice to come home and sleep, stretch out in bed and slide away into sleep.

When the man was about a block away, a car drove up behind him. An arm was extended through the side window of the car and the man fell over.

It wasn't until she saw the man falling that Lucille heard the bang from the shot and realised that in the hand of the outstretched arm there must have been a firearm. It was as if the whole scene was part of a television movie, she had a hard time understanding that she was there in the street and that this happened right in front of her eyes. It was too unreal for that to be true. But it happened, and there was nothing she could do about it.

She felt her stomach suddenly churning at her. It was mostly fear, and maybe a little sympathy. But sympathy wasn't Lucille Meyer's major strength, so it wasn't much of that involved.

The car shrieked away and Lucille looked at the outstretched man. He was lying on his stomach and on the back of his bright suit was a small dark spot. It seemed to be growing all the time, but despite the confusion she felt, she could argue with herself that it was impossible for the stain to grow larger. Blood always flows down, not up. Afterwards, she thought it strange that she thought of such things. But nothing is strange when you get upset.

Lucille turned and ran back the same way she had come. After one or two blocks, she calmed down so much that she could walk at normal pace. She did not want to attract attention, she did not want to be involved in anything. The only thing that really mattered to her was getting away from that shooting as quickly as possible.

It was as if that gunshot had threatened her. As if it had been directed towards her. As if she had been in the middle of the line. She knew it wasn't true, but she was very upset.

She felt the bang from the shot echo through her head; as if it would never end, as if she were to be pursued by that sound for the rest of her life. It was nothing she looked forward to.

There were other things that were similar, things that slowly passed. Maybe she knew what other things, maybe she was not just imagining them. She didn't know for sure, and that was not the most important thing at the moment.

Lucille Meyer fled in some kind of general panic.

Afterwards, she was very disappointed in herself. She didn't want to do things without importance. It was such behavior she despised. But now she had behaved in that awful way.

When she reached Dumain Street and saw Partridge's book shop, she was almost totally calm again. Most of what just happened was at a distance now, it had been a while. She heard the sirens from the police cars, the police warning light looking into all the dark flashes and screams. She sat down with Mr Partridge's accounting again.

In some way she felt even more anxious. It was as if the accounting had been lying in the shop calling for her while she was out in the streets and got startled. She didn't like to be scared, no one does, but for Lucille Meyer it felt like a personal insult. She had lived so long in the firm assurance that she was not easy to frighten.

Now she was scared out of her wits and she didn't like it at all. It was as if someone had been opening the lid of her brain, as if someone had penetrated into her very soul's most private place.

The fear and disappointment made her freeze in the warm night. She was very surprised and very scared, but she wanted to stay, did not want to escape, she wanted to live. Did not want to collapse like a bloodstained bundle on the sidewalk, wanted to live until she reached that other, diffuse life she had dreamed about for so long.

In a way, she felt the old longing for her parents, but

she knew that it was a weakness, a moment of weakness, that would leave her in a few days.

Now it was all about preserving the feeling of life she still had inside her, so that no one came and pawed at it. She wanted to be herself, alone, and knew she could handle it, only people around her did not become too aggressive towards her. Now she felt threatened, but knew it was going to pass, just like all other things pass. Lucille worked in Louisiana's dark night. The night smelled of roses and perfume, charcoal and grilled meat. Lucille did not want to admit that it also smelled of powdery smoke, sweat and blood.

She wanted to forget that part of this night. Accounting through the black night was what she wanted to do now, nothing else. She wanted to forget everything else, whatever was out there in the dark night. She wanted to get away from all that nasty stuff.

She was surprised that the shot had not made a louder pop.

Lucille was 22 years old. It wouldn't have mattered if she had been only 16.

Not Much of a Smile

Some evenings are pure torture, other evenings you want to remember for the rest of your life. Most evenings are just ordinary and you can't remember them afterwards. Some evenings get stuck in your memory, even though you prefer to forget them for good. You don't want any reruns of that very special evening. But memories are a part of life and you have to endure them, whether you like them or not.

Some evenings that get stuck for good in one's consciousness are evenings you would like to repeat, but which you know are impossible to ever relive. Other evenings you prefer to get away from, but it is these evenings that most unequivocally bite into one's memories. What happens at those moments doesn't have to be that weird, or overwhelming. It can start out as a very ordinary evening.

It is a very ordinary evening. The hotel is quiet. A few weeks earlier it was full of congress participants. It was the messy kind of congress. What they really congregated on is no longer remembered. It got messy, that was the lasting impression. But they have long since made their move. It is as if the whole hotel is recovering after that messy ordeal. Dave has done just that anyway. He must try to recover, because that congress was a terrible time.

He can't really believe that people, as soon as they get away from home, have to act like pigs to have fun. He's not even sure they had the nice kind of fun, those congressmen. They may have thought they had, but they didn't look like they were having a good time. But now another reality prevails.

Hotel Dobson welcomes its guests as it have always done. No one asks what the guests do when they are by themselves, as long as the police do not ask for the guests.

Dobson wants peace and quiet. It is not good for business to let it grow too messy, then the serious guests will not come back.

Room 324, a German, calls and wants a beer. Dave tries to explain to him that there is beer in the fridge, in his room.

The German does not understand.

Dave does not know if it is because the German speaks bad English, or if he is all too drunk to understand. It is important to have all possibilities open. Above all, it is important not to be prejudiced!

"Listen now, Mister!" Dave says.

He is impatient, but does not want to show it. At least at the same level he experiences it. It is always bad policy towards the guests to show your irritation with them. After all, it is those guys who pay, and you have to give them quite a lot of leeway, although there are of course boundaries. They must not fall out of the frame.

"There are at least four cold beers in your refrigerator,

Sir, take them out, then we put them on your tab!" Dave says and is sensing how tired he gets to hang out and talk to intoxicated people every night.

He wishes, for one, that the guests could do anything but drink. For example, they could sleep in the hotel, he thinks it is one of the things that you do in a hotel. But apparently the hotel guests do not agree with him.

It's as if all the hotel guests just want to fuck with Dave. Yes, he knows it isn't, but he often feels like they showed up at Dobson solely to drive him to the outer brink of insanity.

He doesn't like it. But he himself has chosen to have this job and must endure it, for a while, at least.

At least it would be like a major defeat to quit since you can't cope with the guests. He could never stand giving in like that.

"I want a beer, a cold!" the German says.

This guy has apparently decided not to let the hotel staff boss him around. It is only acceptable. It is the most difficult part. There are some that seem to be checking in at hotels just to be able to give the staff a hard time. Dave has encountered some specimens in his days, but you forget those things, fortunately. Otherwise you would go crazy!

"Okay," Dave moans.

He surrenders, that guy won't give in until he gets what he wants. Right now Dave has no power to resist. There are days when the energy just runs out of you, you can't stop it. There's nothing stopping it. Suddenly, you discover that there is not enough energy anywhere.

"Good," the German says and sounds pleased.

Anyway, it is great that he stopped sounding so aggressive. Dave has a hard time with people like that, doesn't think they seem real. The whole contradictory garnish always seems so sticky. But, you can never know for sure. Some are probably born that way and then it is simply to pity them. Those who joined in with that style later can only complain. That's not what they need. That is just like a stab in the back.

"I'll be right up with it," Dave says.

He hates going around with the items the guests order, but with this German he has just no choice. Dave opens the small fridge and brings out a Coors. Brings a glass too, though he knows there are three glasses in the German room. He starts his walk with the beer. He had a chance to escape. The German might not let him into the room in the middle of the night.

Maybe the German does mind drinking from the glasses that are on hand in the room. You never know what kid of preferences the guests have. It is exciting, at least when you are rested and do not have to think about staying awake.

Dave has met all kinds of wackos during his time at Dobson. He is no longer surprised, that time is long gone. You are grinding hard during the first months at this job. It is an asset to have met the nutcases, but it is important not to show them that you think they are weird.

Then they become dissatisfied and it is not good for Dobson's reputation. Poor service is what many hotels are known for. They really can't afford that at a place like Dobson.

Just as he is pushing the button to the elevator, the phone rings. He turns on the heel; he is experiencing a wave of irritation well up. Preferably the phone could have called while he was still by the phone! But that's how it always is; as soon as you leave, something stops you!

"Hotel Dobson, the porter!"

Dave doesn't really know how many times he has uttered those words, as if they had finally become some kind of magic spell for him. They now come automatically when he answers a phone. Even when he answers at home, the phrase may slip out of him. He is seriously injured!

"Hi, it's Celia! How's that in the buzzing middle of town, Dave?" she asks in her usual soft voice.

He relaxes right away. Her voice makes him happy. It's like a still lighthouse from the better side of his life. The part of life that is peace and quiet, four walls, a good book and a bottle of wine.

"Unruly, I'm sorry, we have eight rooms available and not a single reservation for tomorrow night. Everyone checks out in the morning ... can you hold a beat, I have to bring a beer to a guest?" he says as he recalls what he was doing when Celia called.

He is glad that he does not forget the German; that guy can cause him a whole lot of trouble if he is not kept happy.

"Okay," Celia sighs.

Dave senses his craving for her when he is listening to her voice. As if she is more attractive, like this, at a distance, even more than when they are in each other's company. A strange experience, but it is there, all the same. It is as if the distance reinforces his longing for her, as if he cannot resist her just because she is not beside him right now.

He smiles inwardly. He always feels intellectual when talking to Celia, she has to infect him with something. He has never felt this way with any woman before. She evokes hidden depths within him. He grimaces and put the handset next to the phone. As he rides up and gets out of the elevator on the third floor, he hears the pigeons rumble behind the broken window next to the fire stairs in the corridor. The pigeons pick on the remaining inner glass pane. That's how it has been as long as he has worked here. Dave has often thought that they should fix the broken pane. But it seems like, all the time, other things come in between.

We have to fix that window, he thinks. At the same time, he is aware of that he will forget the window pane. It's not a great idea to remember it; doubtful if it will be rectified anyway. The level of service is not the highest at Dobson's.

When he knocks on the German's door, it is completely silent on the other side. Dave gets pissed off and knocks a little harder. Nothing is heard this time either.

He wonders if he should knock again, or just place the tray outside the door, but then the guy will refuse to pay. Or come back later and call again, even more aggressive than just now.

Then the door opens with a jerk. Dave shrugs. The German stands there in his briefs staring at Dave with wild eyes and his hair on end. Dave got scared when the door was opened that way. He should have been prepared, but it's like you can never really be.

"Your beer, S-Sir," Dave stutters.

He is annoyed that he stuttered like that. He does not like the rubicund man that towers in front of him. It is as if the German is coming towards him. Dave really doesn't like it.

The German stares at him for a few moments. Then he takes the tray from Dave. He takes it with precision, so Dave thinks he can't be very drunk anyway.

But you never know.

Once they had a guest who downed a quart of gin and seemed so completely calm and nice until they discovered that he jumped out the window.

Then the police came and afterwards it was all in the newspapers about Dobson. What could be read there was not considered good advertising for the hotel. They got a doorman who should try to decide how drunk the guests were. But that's easier said than done. You can't sit with them in their room and see what they pour down into themselves!

"Thanks," the German says, and slams the door behind him again.

The German puts on the safety chain while Dave walks towards the elevator. He is glad that the German does not talk anymore. There are many sad words that have been thrown in the face when you come up with a tray in that manner.

At least he said thank you, Dave reflects, as he stands in the elevator, many don't even do that.

"Now I am done!" Dave tells Celia in the handset.

For a moment, he is afraid that she has hung up at the other end. The handset roars ominously.

"Fine! Honey, can't we meet when you quit?" she wonders breathlessly, in that special way she uses when she's anxious about something.

Dave doesn't ask her what she wants, he assumes that she can't help but meet him. From time to time she is affected by such serious attacks of coercion and closeness and then he usually puts up with it if he is feeling up to it.

"Aren't you going to be unconscious at eight in the morning if you're awake now and calling here?" he wonders.

Celia is a lady who likes to have her eight hours of sleep, otherwise she does not feel well. Dave would also like to sleep eight hours, or at least six hours a day, but he knows he is careless about it. This is probably the explanation to the constant headache in recent years.

"No, that's something I have to talk to you about. Something important, you have to make yourself free if you have something else planned!"

"Okay, where are we going to meet?"

Dave doesn't even bother to ask what it is suddenly so important.

He vaguely thinks that she has not received her period in time and believes she is pregnant. It has happened before and she is very excited about that stuff.

"Down at Statley's on Pacific Avenue?"

At first, Dave doesn't know what place she is talking about.

"At the metro station?" he asks as he recalls that they had met at that place some time earlier.

It has the advantage of being convenient for them, being situated halfway between her apartment and Dobson's Hotel.

"Yes," she answers and he can hear her breathing.

She sounds breathless, as if she's been running to the phone. Maybe she is doing her yoga or something and has found out that she has to call him?

"Okay, then we'll meet there, about a quarter past eight," Dave says, and is about to hang up.

He stops at the last moment, because Celia belongs to the group of people who have made it a great art to come up with the most important thing they want to say just as you end the conversation.

"Good, bye! Take care!"

A snapping sound is coming out of the handset and he is sure she's said what she wants to say. For now.

Dave is hearing her hanging up. Of course he's wondering what she wants to talk to him about. It is strange that she is awake at half past two at night. Why didn't she call earlier? But you can never know for certain with Celia.

Suddenly she might wake up in the middle of the

night and want to discuss something that can't wait until morning. What she has got into her head she have to implement immediately. Sure it's charming, but hard in the long run too.

Dave strolls into the room behind the front desk. He takes a beer out of the fridge and puts a dollar in the box next to the fridge. He jerks at the sharp sound as he opens the can. The beer produces some froth when Dave rips open the can and the foam bubbles out of it. He swiftly puts the can to his mouth and takes a few quick gulps. When he looks at the clock on the wall it is exactly a quarter in two. There is something strange about it. As if it was important that she'd be a quarter to two. He can't understand why.

It seems to become a long night.

He reclines on the sofa in the back room and begins reading. He has brought a book by Isaac Bashevis Singer. It's called "Enemies. A Love Story." Just the title was enough to get him to buy it. Then he found out that the Singer was famous. Dave loses himself in the story of Herman Broder and his three wives.

When Dave wakes up it is half past five. The phone is ringing. He rushes to answer. He immediately recognises the German. This time he sounds even more drunk and upset. He wants another beer.

Dave sighs, now he knows that this German can be awkward, since now he has either drunk all his alcohol, or slept and woken up with a hangover. Both variants are equally cumbersome to deal with.

"Okay, I'm coming!"

He takes a beer and for safety a glass, then he is riding the elevator. He is hearing music and a voice trying to sing along to that music coming from the German's room. But things are not going very well. The melody doesn't really match the lyrics. Dave knocks on the German's door. The German opens the door in the same wild way as before. He is still only wearing briefs. But now he has a whiskey glass in one hand. Dave sees a row of small liquor bottles and empty beer cans of the brand found in the fridge in the room.

"Cheers!" the German says before taking the beer from the tray and slamming the door shut again.

The whole scene passes lightning fast and Dave is happy that the German did not threaten him in any way, but chose to disappear into his room. It went well this time too and he is grateful for that.

You will get a surprise in the morning when you pay the bill and you have to pay for all those bottles, Dave thinks. But that is not strictly his concern, he does not let it weigh him down very much.

He rides the elevator down and goes in and lies down on the sofa again.

He only wakes up when Bert wakes him shortly after seven.

"The hotel is on fire!" Bert hollers.

Dave swings himself up from the couch hearing Bert's loud laugh.

"How's the night been? I guess all the guests have disappeared with all the towels and sheets while you were sleeping!" Bert laughs.

"Really hope not, but the guy in 324 has consumed his mini bar, you better check carefully before letting him leave."

"Then he might wake up late, I reckon," Bert says, checking that all the stuff is in the usual places.

"Yes, okay, nothing else has really happened, so we'll better start breakfast," Dave, says and yawns.

He feels terrible. He wonders if his headaches are malign, feels like he has a hangover, even though he hasn't been drinking much for at least a month.

"Let's do that!"

Bert takes Dave's seat on the couch. Dave starts making coffee and brings out the dry muffins from the fridge.

"Now I'll call it a day," Dave says.

Admittedly, he's supposed to be at Dobson until eight sharp, but it's not exactly a rush, he might as well take off if Bert doesn't mind.

"Right on, man," Bert laughs.

Bert laughs a lot. Dave doesn't think he himself can handle being that perky every morning. But, Bert is just like that when Dave releases him late at night.

So Bert may simply be a happy man. He always laughs, and Dave himself doesn't do that very often. Not as often as he himself would like anyway. Dave meets one of the room cleaners as he leaves. They greet each other. Her name is Katy, Dave knows that, but he rarely sees her.

Not that he is particularly interested in her, but he sometimes regrets meeting so few people. He very rarely have regrets, he likes this job because he doesn't have to see so many people around him. Yes, and there are guests then, but they all come new all the time. So there is some kind of change there as well.

*

At Statley's, Celia is waiting with a glass of ice water and a cup of coffee. She is slowly puffing on a menthol cigarette. Her blonde hair looks a little streaky, but after all, the light from the cafeteria window makes it shine a little.

Dave waves to her through the window and steps into the café.

"Good morning!"

Dave sits down opposite her. She looks up quickly, with a flickering gaze. She looks very tired, as if she has been sleeping very badly.

"Haven't you slept at all?" Dave wonders, taking her hand and caressing it.

"No," she answers tonelessly.

He is already worried, just listening to her voice. Now he suspects that she has already received all the answers to the tests and everything is definitive.

"Why?"

But Celia often has problems with stuff like this, which is why Dave learned not to ask her anything straight up. Celia thinks this is burdensome and rude.

"Dave, there's something I have to tell you," she says abruptly, as if she's been in it for a long time, as if she really wants to come out with it.

"Yes, yes."

Celia seems so different. Not only does her voice sound strange, it is as if she is a completely different person than usual.

"Jack called last night."

She glances at him with a few anxious looks.

That Jack called her should have warned him, but he is not really upset after working all night. Sure, he has also slept some, but there is never anything quite like really sleeping.

You are resting at full alert all the time.

"Well, what did he want?"

"He told me your mother is dead."

Dave will always remember that toneless voice mode she uses. It is as if she does not really want to participate in what she has to say to him.

"Oh."

It's as if it takes him a while to grasp what she's saying. He should just ask what she said when he fully realises that his mother is dead. He has always known that this moment would come sooner or later, but it does not matter, he is completely unprepared.

"Are you sad?"

He doesn't like that she feels sorry for him. He simply doesn't want her to.

"A little, but it was not unexpected."

He even feels so tired that he could sleep for a few days at a time. It is as if all his stamina has left him.

"Dave, how are you doing?"

He gives her a bored glance and sighs.

140

"It works out well, I was certainly more taken than I could have anticipated."

Dave laughs pale faced towards Celia.

"Shall we leave?" she wonders and collects her stuff.

"Yes."

Vandelier's song

It had been raining that entire afternoon. Usually he liked the rain. But now it was probably the third, or possibly the fourth day, that it was pouring down. Vandelier had not realised that there could be so much rain left after the first day. This morning he had woken up with a strange feeling that something was really wrong. It was the first time in a long time.

He had been spared from such premonitions for a long time, but now it was time. He had even begun to enjoy the hotel he was staying at. Not because there was much to enjoy. If you wanted to be kind, it was a hotel where gallant ladies were paid to let less gallant gentlemen pat them on the behind.

It was a kind of service facility, where the ladies were not ladies and the gallant just showed in the late habits of all the women. But it suited Vandelier quite well. He had nothing to complain about. The ladies did not disturb him and as far as he knew he did nothing to disturb them.

There was a kind of mutual low-key truce between them. It was as if the ladies had understood what kind of guy he was as soon as he showed up at that place. He was grateful for that.

They did not care for him and he did not contact them,

they lived side by side, but none of them suffered. It worked out just fine.

He had a snack at a bar near the hotel and then set out on a real long walk. He had even jogged a few blocks to get the heart pumping.

Vandelier imagined that this would be good for him. He thought he could benefit from a little more fitness in his life. He was a little surprised at his own efforts. He was for first time in his life interested in tomorrow. It was a pretty uplifting sensation for a guy like George Vandelier.

It's been a long time since he thought about tomorrow. Vandelier was not the only one to deal with that, but he still had a hard time getting his own thoughts and actions to become one. He thought in a certain manner, and knew that you had to be tough to get through, but rarely dared to be as tough as he knew he ought to be. That was his dilemma.

He felt like he was completely renovating himself. He didn't really understand what was happening to him. Since he took the last glass he had become totally changed. He did not recognise himself. But it wasn't just bad. He felt pretty good, he has to admit that. To his great dismay, he found that he liked this kind of life. He would never have believed that if someone had told him about it a few years ago. It had been a long time since he had felt so good. In addition, he had quite fun, got to do what he was best at, and did not need to do a lot of chores on the side.

For the first time in a very long time, Vandelier felt

quite satisfied with himself. It amused him a lot. During the five weeks Vandelier had worked at Crazy Cradle, he had not tasted a drop. He had revived an old habit of never drinking while working.

Vandelier thrived at Crazy Cradle. Of course, there were some time between the moments when someone asked him to play something by Mozart or Wagner, but he was used to it after all these years at the piano.

Cole Porter and Bernstein were often requested, as well as songs that Sinatra made popular. Vandelier didn't mind playing them. He liked to play everything, if he could caress the keys it didn't matter what the audience wanted to hear. He loved the feeling when his fingertips touched the keys and pressed them down. The feeling when the right tone, just long enough and rightly accentuated, sounds from the piano has always been his greatest impetus to play.

He could sit alone and play. If only he got paid for it, it wouldn't matter to him that no one listened to him. The gig at Crazy Cradle was the first one he had had in over a year. Last summer he had to work in a bus garage. He had been vacuuming and washing buses for six months.

Then he had saved up enough to manage for a few months on his own. It was the first time he had managed to reach a goal in recent years. He was very proud of it. It had been a wonderful feeling. At that moment it had been quite a long time since he had completely disposed of his time on his own.

He walked the streets and felt like a king some days.

144

It was wonderful not having to answer to anyone other than yourself.

He had become his own boss and it suited him just fine, he didn't even bother to ask himself for advice. He hadn't done much in those months. He had been drinking some, but quite restrained. He had never lost his footing. He had played for free at bars, just for the feeling of being able to play.

He had a pretty good life. He had even thought it was quite sad to drink and had increasingly pulled down the ration. Not that he got completely dry, but compared to his drinking in earlier days, there was a significant difference.

A new Vandelier had begun to emerge during those months. He was very surprised. He hadn't really expected it. He had simply believed that he was a has-been, that he would never be able to play like he used to. But it turned out that it was not too late, it only took a little time.

He had never experienced time as a threat. He had never been afraid of time itself. What scared him about time was the importance that other people put on it. They seemed to think it was a kind of reality, that time itself really was something.

He had never really been able to understand that way of looking at it.

Before the money ran out, he had managed to get a temporary job as a bartender in a joint. It was the kind of job he had had many times during his life. In addition, a job he had mastered quite well! Not that it mattered to the regular customers, but Vandelier was a contender mixing drinks.

There was something about the blending of drinks that had a relationship with the feeling of playing the piano. He didn't exactly know what, but rarely did he waste his time mixing the eighth Tom Collins that night.

It had its meaning too.

Not only did people get drunk from drinking what he mixed, there was even some kind of aesthetic experience in making those drinks, something that was very similar to sitting at the piano. He just couldn't put his finger on what.

Vandelier wasn't much of a complainer; he tried to make time to play, that was the whole thing. As long as he got a fair amount of time playing music, the rest of his everyday life was no bigger problem for him.

He did not care what it looked like where he lived, what food he ate and so on. If only he got the opportunity to play, then everything else was just paraphernalia.

Those who frequented the bar mostly ordered beer and whiskey. In that order. Some days they probably drank white spirit since there were long periods when some of them did not show up as usual in their chairs at the counter.

And once they came in, they were hanging at the counter until Vandelier closed. He didn't like to be a bartender, even though he liked to mix drinks. But of course it was because he just liked to play the piano. Everything else was just a way to pass the time, and at best to stay alive until the piano gigs showed up.

No, now this was better. Vandelier was kind of happy. Bronowski, the owner was happy, it seemed that Vandelier attracted some customers with his piano playing. The bartender was glad that he had noticed that the tip money was getting more plentiful during the hours Vandelier was playing. Vandelier himself also received some notes in addition to the few that Bronowski paid him. It seemed to grow into a long, fine relationship.

Especially since Vandelier did not drink a drop. He was as dry as a desert.

"Nice day today, right, Vandelier?" Bronowski asked when his pianist arrived at the bar that day.

As usual, Vandelier came in well in advance. He always took his time before work began. He let his fingers get a push with scales and other limbering exercises.

"Yes, really," Vandelier replied.

He did not lie, he thought it was a great day, even though it was the most common cliché. He smiled a little at Bronowski, who smiled back. Vandelier was pleased that Bronowski appeared to be such a cultivated man.

Or, it could also be that he left Vandelier to do what he had hired him to do; to play the piano. Bronowski was simply a pro.

"Want something to drink, Van?" the bartender wondered, as he had just finished wiping off the bar counter.

He was no bartender to Vandelier's taste, but you

can't get everything. He did not like that slick type, perhaps because they reminded him of his father. That was no fond memory.

"Just some tonic," Vandelier said, sitting down on one of the barstools next to Bronowski.

There was plenty of room at the bar, so it didn't matter much if he sat there for a while. Bronowski did not seem to mind either.

"You don't drink much? It's weird, most people who have played here before haven't frowned upon drinking," Bronowski said.

Bronowski took a cautious sip of the whiskey he always took before entering the office to begin the afternoon's work.

"Can't drink, doctor's order, besides, I play better without," Vandelier smiled.

He wasn't really happy with that smile, but you can't be happy all the time, it's just idiots who are, he thought.

"The way you play, you deserve something to drink," the bartender said, smiling with his perfect white teeth towards them.

Those teeth must have cost him a lot, but it wasn't Vandelier's business what the bartender did with his money.

"Tonic is fine with me," Vandelier said.

Vandelier sat down harder on one of the stools at the bar counter and supported his elbows against the counter. He mostly avoided sitting that way, because it wore too much on the jacket's elbows. But once is never and twice is a damn habit, he thought.

"Sure, have whatever you wish!" Bronowski smiled and patted him encouragingly on the shoulder.

Bronowski had a paternal appearance that had no relation to his age, he was probably ten years younger than Vandelier, but in that manner he probably handled all his employees.

Vandelier liked Bronowski.

They sat silent for a while. Vandelier lapped at his tonic. He brought the glass away to the piano. It was always the same ritual, that glass he had not managed to get rid of.

Even if he had succeeded in changing the contents of it, the glass would always go with him to the piano. Nobody objected. At least not Vandelier.

"If you don't mind, Mr. Bronowski, I'll play some warm-up," Vandelier said.

He opened the lid above the keyboard; the white and black keys shone in the dim lighting of the bar.

"Go along," Bronowski muttered.

Vandelier started playing. As soon as his fingers touched the keys, it seemed like he was completely lost to the outside world. He wobbled a bit with the music.

Vandelier was glad that he had managed to work away from his humming to the songs. He had met a lot of trouble with it in the past. Especially when he was married. He had swamped gigs in some finer places because of that undisciplined whining. His crooning didn't have much to do with the tune he was playing. Vandelier was no witch master at singing, but he could play the piano for real. Skilled, very skilled.

He could not stay in tune when he started to sing. He had practiced it, thought it seemed strange that he could not sing, since he could play.

But he had abandoned the idea of singing after listening to a tape recording he made with himself.

There had been no uplifting feeling that passed through him as he listened to that tape.

Just then, he thought he might as well have been able to avoid wasting magnetic tape on it.

After that experience he just played. Playing the piano was som kind of substitute for Vandelier's lack of spiritual talent. He liked those smoky and dark rooms he usually played in. No one knew him, he had to be at peace. And peace was what he wanted most of all. He no longer had any longing for for fame, or even big money.

It was as if that opportunity had been denied him for all time to come.

"But, isn't it George Vandelier?" he heard a voice behind him.

He was at once too scared to turn around. He heard at once in that voice that it was his past standing there behind him in some form.

"George, it's me, Jenny, Madge's sister!"

Vandelier turned around and looked at a woman in her 40s. He immediately recognised her. In the dim light, she reminded him a lot of Madge. Far too much really.

"How on earth did you end up in a joint like this?" the well-dressed and still pretty slim Jenny wondered.

Her hair still had the same amber color as back in the days. Her eyes were equally brown. As if they never stopped burning with that fire. The fire, which he discovered way too late to enjoy.

"Life put me in this seat, Jenny," George Vandelier said.

He had not interrupted his playing. The scales had so far occupied his fingers. They found the way of their own accord and he was very happy that his fingers had not abandoned him. He was happy with his playing, but thought he could learn to talk a little better. It sounded like something from a century-old book as soon as he opened his mouth, he thought. But he had to live with that.

"But George! In a place like this?" she wondered, raising her well-picked eyebrows. Jenny had always spent a lot of time looking proper, as she called it.

Vandelier didn't think there was anything wrong with that, but Jenny was one of those women, who will have big problems when the time has come and the body wants to get closer to the ground before her heart stops beating.

He felt a little sorry for her regarding that, but it was really nothing he or anyone else, except a skilled plastic surgeon, could do about it. And then only for a short while.

"I hardly think I can sit in on a concert scene nowadays, Jenny," Vandelier said.

He wondered why they always wanted him to do things he didn't want, that he didn't feel comfortable with, things that were foreign to him. It was as if they just couldn't stop holding on to him.

"But, couldn't you give lessons? You have so much to give to others," Jenny said.

She tossed her head in the same way his wife used to do. Once upon a time he had found that certain movement irresistible, but now it was almost annoying. In any case, it did not get to him.

"I'd rather do it here among people who appreciate what I do," he said.

He felt that he would not be able to talk to Jenny for much longer without becoming mean.

He didn't want her to remember him as angry anytime earlier. But it didn't matter. Not at all.

"But! In a bar! You, who used to …"

She stopped herself. As if she now thought she was clinging on too much. As if she said too much. Vandelier looked at her, frankly no longer recognising her.

The past had gotten a completely different face than he had expected!

But he should have expected that it could end this way, and that in the future it would be repeated and end this way many more times. He now realised what he had to prepare for.

"If you think I should regard myself as too good to play in such a place, it probably says more about your attitude to ordinary people than it does about me," Vandelier muttered.

He sighed silently, recognising this discussion from the past, being so tired of it. He could by all means run it in his sleep, so it really didn't matter that it was appearing again.

"You're bitter. But Madge had no choice. You didn't make any money, she simply had to divorce you."

Jenny didn't look like she liked to tell him that, but maybe she had no choice either. She couldn't keep quiet about meeting him anyway, so it was just as good.

"I'm not bitter," George said, "if you want me to cope, don't tell Madge that I'm playing here!"

He looked at her seriously, but had no real clue if she thought his argument was true. He didn't really understand what she was thinking. Maybe it was no idea at all to try to influence her. Perhaps his race was as run as he once thought it to be.

"I like you, but I can't do that to my own sister, she needs money," Jenny sighed.

She shrugged, as if to tell him that she would have acted differently had she not been a sister of Madge's. But now her hands were tied, so to speak.

"Yes, who doesn't," Vandelier said.

He switched into playing another tune. It was a way to avoid what was coming, but there were a lot of other ways too. The sad thing was that this way was the only thing he was really good at. All the other ways there were a lot of others being good at.

"Bye George," Jenny said, looking at him for a long time before she left.

Vandelier did not look at her leaving. He had looked at her back so many times that he knew what it was like to see her leave a room.

He left it to the others in the room, to those who had not seen the spectacle before, to look at her from behind. Vandelier played for a while. Then he got up abruptly and walked up to Bronowski, who was still sitting at the bar.

Vandelier experienced that the distance between the bar and the piano had at least tripled in the last 15 minutes. Vandelier shook his head.

"Bad news?" Bronowski wondered, looking at Vandelier with brown, attentive eyes.

Vandelier got the impression that this was the first time Bronowski had really seen him.

"The past," Vandelier said, and was very serious, probably had never been more serious in his entire life.

He knew the past all too well and now it had gotten grips on him.

"Something to drink?" the bartender wondered.

He thoughtfully looked at Vandelier, as if he were looking at him for the first time, or as if he were seeing the real George Vandelier for the first time. There might not have been any major difference between the Vandelier who came in a while ago and the man who was standing in front of the bartender now. But there was a difference, he noticed.

"A shot of gin," Vandelier said.

He lit a cigarette, felt for a little smoke right now, it would be nice to have a drink too. It had been a long time since he had felt such a craving for a cigarette. It was as if he had not smoked for years.

Bronowski looked with growing astonishment at him

as Vandelier walked towards the piano with the glass in his hand. There was another man who was walking there now, a completely different man than the one who entered Crazy Cradle an hour ago. Vandelier had changed and it was very sinister.

During the weeks Vandelier had worked at the bar, he had kept himself clean. He used an old habit of never drinking while working. Vandelier thrived at Crazy Cradle.

Of course, there were eons of time between the times when someone asked him to play something by Mozart or Wagner. But Mozart or Wagner are not all that is important in the world, he had learned that lesson the hard way.

Bronowski sighed, now it was probably time to start looking for a new pianist. He smiled a little palely at the bartender, had a sip from his glass and disappeared into his office.

At the piano, Vandelier sat down with his glass. It was no longer just an decoration on the lid of the piano. Now it was a real glass again. Vandelier looked a little forlorn. But he played on as usual. It was just one difference compared to yesterday.

Vandelier started humming.

Now he was crooning.

Post Script

The major part of these eleven short stories was written during a month's travels with the coaches of the Greyhound lines during the fall of 1979. Starting in Connecticut, going via New Orleans, to Houston where my partner and me caught a flight to Mexico City, staying there for a half a week. Then riding the coach run by *Autobuses Chihuahuenses* the 24 hour ride up to Ciudad Juarez – El Paso, to continue our travels towards the coast of California. We went eastward on a more northern trail. Our last stop before returning to Connecticut was Montreal, Canada.

During our four weeks of travelling with Greyhound, sleeping on the buses, checking in to cheap hotels, speaking to strangers, hanging out in coffee shops, checking out the stuff to watch, looking at life around us, watching television and reading newspapers, we were exposed to a lot of stories. Some of them became this book. Others belong in a different book.